THE YOUNGERMAN GUNS

THE YOUNGERMAN GUNS

Lewis B. Patten

Chivers Press • G.K. Hall & Co.
Bath, England   Thorndike, Maine USA

This Large Print edition is published by Chivers Press, England, and by G.K. Hall & Co., USA.

Published in 1999 in the U.K. by arrangement with Golden West Literary Agency.

Published in 1999 in the U.S. by arrangement with Golden West Literary Agency.

U.K. Hardcover ISBN 0–7540–3649–9 (Chivers Large Print)
U.K. Softcover   ISBN 0–7540–3650–2 (Camden Large Print)
U.S. Softcover   ISBN 0–7838–0446–6 (Nightingale Series Edition)

The text of this Large Print edition is unabridged.
Other aspects of the book may vary from the original edition.

Set in 16 pt. New Times Roman.

Printed in Great Britain on acid-free paper.

British Library Cataloguing in Publication Data available

Library of Congress Cataloging-in-Publication Data

Patten, Lewis B.
     The Youngerman guns / Lewis B. Patten.
        p.   cm.
    ISBN 0–7838–0446–6 (lg. print : sc : alk. paper)
    1. Large type books.   I. Title.
    [PS3566.A79Y68   1999]
    813'.54—dc21   98–48525

CHAPTER ONE

There were crickets chirping over on Elm Street in the tall cottonwoods, and there were children yelling as they played hide-and-seek in the warm, early dusk of June. Main Street was quiet along most of its length but at the lower end, half a block above the depot, the Free State Saloon made an isolated spot of yellow lamplight and of talk that came from the swinging doors as an indistinguishable babble, almost a steady hum.

Dan Youngerman sat in a straight-backed chair tilted against the front wall of the stone-block jail, a pipe firmly clenched between his teeth. There was a faint frown on his forehead as he stared along the street. Something had made him uneasy today, something so vague he couldn't decide what it had been.

Dobeville, Kansas, was the county seat. Around it sprawled a rich and rolling country of farms and ranches and of land as yet unoccupied by either, where even yet an occasional buffalo was seen. Dobeville wasn't wild like Dodge City and Wichita. It was quiet and settled and prosperous. Dobeville didn't even have a town marshal, relying instead on the sheriff to keep the peace. Dan Youngerman was the sheriff's deputy.

There had always been a lot of joshing about

his name. They said it was some joke to have a Youngerman as the sheriff's deputy. Dan always grinned amiably when they joked about his name and so far he had managed to pass it off successfully. Not even Luke Smead, the sheriff, suspected that he really was related to the Wilkeses and the Youngermans. If he had suspected, Dan knew he wouldn't have a job. Not in Dobeville or anyplace else. The Wilkes-Youngerman gang was the most notorious gang of border outlaws that the recent war had spawned. There was a price of five thousand dollars on the head of Sam Youngerman and lesser amounts on the members of the gang.

Sam was Dan's oldest brother and the leader of the gang. Dan hadn't seen him for more than seven years and he didn't want to see him. Never again.

Down at the lower end of Main, a man appeared from between two buildings. He briefly hesitated in front of the Free State Saloon, then went inside. Suddenly Dan knew why he had felt so uneasy all day today. He must have glimpsed this same man earlier. The same vague resemblance that troubled him now must have troubled him before, except that he hadn't realized it. The stranger looked like Hugh Wilkes, one of his cousins from Arkansas and a member of the Wilkes-Youngerman gang.

Dan brought his chair forward suddenly. He stood up and headed for the saloon at a rapid walk. Halfway there he stopped. If the man was Hugh, he didn't want to go barging into the saloon where Wilkes, startled, might give him away. He and Sarah had seven years of their lives invested here. They had successfully put the violence and hatred of the war years behind. They had a son six years old and a daughter four. They had a place in the community.

The frown deepened on Dan Youngerman's brow. What was Hugh doing in Dobeville anyway? Western Kansas was a long way from the gang's usual operating area. Was it possible that he knew his cousin Dan was here? Or did he just happen to be passing through?

Cautiously Dan approached the saloon. He paused on the walk in front and stared through one of the dirty windows. The man he had glimpsed was Hugh all right. He was standing at the bar arguing with Frank Delaney, who worked on a ranch ten miles south of town.

Dan backed away. He stood in the shadows a moment while he repacked and relighted his pipe. His hands were unsteady. Panic briefly touched his thoughts. Hugh could ruin him with a word. If Hugh knew he was here . . .

He shook his head irritably. Hugh couldn't ruin him without ruining himself. If Hugh told who Dan was, he'd have to tell who he was too.

He began to breathe easier. He grinned nervously to himself as he realized how tense he had become. He turned and headed back uptown toward the sheriff's office in the jail.

The shots behind him were muffled, but there was no doubt about where they had been fired. Dan whirled and ran toward the saloon, which he had left only moments before. There was no help for it now. He had to go in and take the chance that Hugh Wilkes would inadvertently give him away. He had no other choice.

He burst through the swinging doors and stopped just inside, his gun drawn and ready in his hand. He stared around at the occupants of the place, who seemed frozen with shock and surprise.

Frank Delaney still stood at the bar but now there was a revolver in his hand. Hugh Wilkes lay on his back in the middle of the floor. His gun was also in his hand.

Dan said, 'Put it away, Frank,' and watched the ranch hand holster the smoking gun. He crossed to Wilkes, and knelt quickly at his side.

Hugh's eyes were open. There was instant recognition in them as he stared up at Dan. There was a spreading spot of blood on the front of his faded shirt. He was shot close to the heart and Dan realized instantly that he didn't have long to live.

Dan didn't speak. Above him Frank said, 'He pulled his gun on me. What was I supposed to do, let him shoot me without trying to defend myself?'

Hugh's eyes shocked Dan because they were

4

so filled with hate. Then they went blank and Hugh was dead. His chest was still.

For an instant Dan couldn't move. His first feeling was one of relief because Hugh had died without giving him away. Then he thought, 'He knew I was here! He wasn't a damn bit surprised when he saw me looking down at him! It was like he was waiting for me to come!'

He got slowly to his feet and looked at Frank. 'He's dead.'

'Oh my God!' Delaney's face was white with shock. 'I didn't mean to kill him! I never killed anybody before. But he drew on me. He didn't give me any choice!'

'What were you arguing about?'

Delaney said, 'The war. I know it sounds foolish because the war's been over more'n seven years, but it's what we were arguing about.' He paused a moment, then added, 'He started it. Gib and I were just talking about the President. He started ranting about what a son-of-a-bitch Grant was.'

The bartender, Gib Duncan, said, 'He's right, Dan. The stranger started it. He was pretty bitter considering how long the war's been over with. The way he talked, it was like it was only yesterday.'

Dan's mouth firmed. They hadn't forgotten and maybe they never would. They couldn't or wouldn't put the war years behind. They were still fighting, justifying their raiding and

5

robbing and killing by citing atrocities committed by Union troops during the war and immediately afterward. But it wasn't all one-sided. The Youngermans and the Wilkeses had ridden with Quantrill and with other border guerrilla troops. They had done some brutal things themselves.

Dan himself had ridden for a while with Quantrill. But by the time the war was over, he was sick of the killing and suffering and violence. He'd only wanted to go home and live in peace.

He looked around at the faces of the townsmen. 'Somebody get a wagon or buckboard. Haul him down to Smitherman's.' Smitherman was the town's undertaker, who ran an undertaking business in conjunction with his furniture store.

A man hurried from the saloon. Dan glanced around again. 'Anybody know who he was? Anybody ever see him before?'

Ned Winslow, the teller in the bank, said, 'He was in the bank this afternoon.'

Dan glanced quickly at him. 'What'd he want in the bank?' He tried to keep the sharpness out of his voice, tried to keep it casual.

'He changed some gold coin into currency. A couple of hundred dollars worth.'

Dan nodded. He waited uneasily and after several minutes heard a wagon rattle to a halt outside. He said, 'Two or three of you pick him

6

up and carry him to the wagon.'

Several of the men raised the body and carried it outside. They laid it in the wagon bed. Dan went to the side of the wagon and emptied the dead man's pockets. There was a sweat-stained wallet full of currency and a coin purse containing a couple of keys and a few loose coins. Outside of a worn-looking pocketknife with one broken blade, there was nothing else. He dropped the articles in his side coat pocket, nodded at the driver, and the wagon creaked away. A couple of the men who had carried the body out sat on the tail gate so they could help carry it into the undertaker's.

Dan watched until the wagon was out of sight. Behind him in the saloon the babble of excited voices went on. Other townsmen drifted down the street, having heard the commotion and come to see what it was all about.

Dan knew now why Hugh Wilkes had come to Dobeville. Sam's hatred finally got the better of him. Because he knew he couldn't kill his brother outright, he was going to raid Dobeville and rob the bank. He'd do worse if the townspeople gave him any fight.

Dan turned and headed dispiritedly toward his office. Frank Delaney came out of the saloon and caught up with him. 'What are you going to do about me, Dan? Do I have to stand trial for killing him?'

Dan glanced at Frank, frowning to himself.

7

He shook his head. 'You could if you insisted on being cleared, I suppose, but I don't see any use in it. A dozen men saw what happened. They all say it was self-defense. As far as I'm concerned, that's the end of it. I'm pretty sure the sheriff will feel that way too.'

'Whatever you say, Dan. It makes a man feel awful, though, killing another man like that. Maybe it doesn't bother you. You were in the war. But it sure does bother me.'

Dan said, 'It still bothers me.' He was thinking that Frank would have a lot more to worry about if Sam and the others found out he was the one who had killed Hugh.

Frank veered away and stood on the other side of the street a moment, hesitating. Dan went on to the sheriff's office. He opened the door and stepped inside. He lighted a lamp after trimming the wick, then closed the door and crossed the room to his desk.

Hugh Wilkes had obtained the information Sam wanted, but he wasn't going to get back with it. That meant Sam would have to send someone else to get the information he needed before he could make his raid.

Any way a man looked at it, it meant trouble for Dobeville. It meant trouble for Dan and for Sarah and the children too. Maybe, he thought, he ought to leave. Maybe he ought to take Sarah and the two kids and get out of town. If he wasn't here, there'd be no reason for Sam to raid Dobeville.

8

But he didn't believe it. Hugh had been killed here. Dan and Sarah had been accepted by the people here. Sam wouldn't need any more reasons than that.

And once Sam made up his mind to do something, nothing on earth was going to turn him aside. He *would* raid Dobeville. That was as certain as sunrise tomorrow. What Dan had to decide was how he was going to stop it without throwing away the last seven years of his life, and maybe the next twenty years of it as well.

CHAPTER TWO

At ten, Dan got stiffly to his feet. He blew out the lamp and crossed the room to the door. He locked it behind him and stared down the street. The commotion caused by the shooting earlier had quieted. The saloon was still open but most of its patrons had gone home.

Dan walked reluctantly toward his house a block off Main. The kids would be in bed but Sarah would be waiting up. She waited up every night. He dreaded to tell her it was Hugh Wilkes who had been killed in the saloon tonight because she would guess, as quickly as he had, what Hugh's presence in town meant in terms of trouble for the two of them. She would realize that Sam had picked Dobeville

9

to raid. And she would know why.

In front of the house he paused. A lamp was burning in the living room. Frowning, he walked on past. Maybe if he had a little more time to compose himself, he wouldn't have to tell her. Maybe she didn't even need to know.

The air was warm. Crickets chirped and a faint breeze stirred the leaves of the cottonwoods. After thinking it over, he admitted it wouldn't be fair to keep the dead man's identity from her, because then she wouldn't know Sam and the rest of them were coming to raid the bank. And besides, she'd see he was worried even if he didn't tell her about Hugh. He wouldn't be able to conceal that from her.

He stopped across from the depot, filled and lighted his pipe. He stared gloomily at the light burning in the telegrapher's office. Luke Smead, the sheriff, ought to be back tomorrow. He supposed he'd have to tell Luke who the dead man was. But how would he explain his ability to recognize a member of the Youngerman gang?

He admitted that he owed it to Luke to tell him the entire truth. About who he was. About why he figured Sam Youngerman was going to raid the bank. He ought to make the offer to resign.

But he knew that he would not. Not yet at least. He could be dead wrong about Sam's intentions. Maybe Hugh had just happened to be passing through.

There would be plenty of time to tell the sheriff if and when Sam sent somebody else to scout the bank. If another member of the gang showed up in town, then he'd know for sure what Sam's intentions were.

He walked back toward home. He could hold off telling the sheriff who the dead man was, but he couldn't conceal the truth from Sarah. She had a right to know if Sam was threatening their security.

The house they lived in was a white frame house with a big lilac bush on the south side of the porch. Morning-glory vines climbed on trellises on both sides of the steps. Dan's boots sounded hollowly on the porch. He opened the screen door and went inside.

Sarah sat in a platform rocker, a lamp on the table at her side. She was mending a pair of young Danny's pants. She looked up, a quiet smile appearing on her face.

Hers was a pretty face, but showing a few lines now around the eyes and mouth. He liked her appearance though—even more now than when he had married her.

Because they were so close, she knew immediately that something was wrong. Her eyes questioned him and when he didn't say anything, she asked, 'What were the gunshots about downtown?'

'A killing in the saloon.' He sailed his hat at the coat tree and it caught and stayed. He sank

11

down on the sofa and leaned forward, staring at her. 'The dead man was Hugh Wilkes.'

For an instant she stared blankly at him, slow to comprehend. Then the blood drained out of her face. Her eyes took on a trapped, almost frantic look. 'Hugh? What was he doing here?'

'Maybe nothing. Maybe he was just passing through.'

'You know better than that. The Youngermans and the Wilkeses never just "happen" to be doing anything. Sam has found us, hasn't he? And he's going to raid Dobeville to ruin us?'

'Maybe not. Anyway, Hugh is dead so if Sam sent him here to scout the bank, he still doesn't know any more about it than he did before. He'll have to send someone else.'

'We should have changed our name.'

He met her eyes with his own steady ones. 'I guess we should have, but it's too late now. He knows where we are.'

'Can't we leave? Can't we go away—before Sam even realizes Hugh is dead?'

'We could but that wouldn't stop Sam. Hugh's been killed here in Dobeville. He'd raid it now, even if we weren't here. No, I figure we've got to stay, or at least that I do. I owe that much to the people here.'

'If you stay, then I'll stay too.'

He got up and crossed the room to her. He stood looking down. 'I'd rather you went away.

12

We could say your mother or sister was sick or something.'

She shook her head stubbornly and he realized that she wouldn't go. He said, 'You know what will happen if Sam does raid the bank and if he gets away with it, don't you?'

She nodded. 'They'll say you were part of it. They'll say you sent word to him about the bank and the town. You'll never be able to convince them otherwise. They'll send you to prison.'

Frowning, Dan began to pace back and forth, occasionally pausing to stare moodily outside at the summer darkness in the street. 'Why couldn't he just let us alone? You'd think he'd eventually get over something that happened more than seven years ago.'

'Not Sam. He never gets over anything.' There was bitterness in her voice.

Dan heard the sound of footsteps on the porch and glanced warily at the door. Then he grinned wryly at his own nervousness. He had half-expected to see Sam Youngerman standing there, beard and six-shooter and all. But it was Sheriff Smead. The sheriff said, 'I was hoping you'd still be up. I want to talk to you.'

Sam opened the screen door and the sheriff came inside. He was dusty and unshaven and it was obvious he had just returned. He'd ridden over to the northeast corner of the county yesterday to serve some papers and he hadn't expected to be back until tomorrow.

Dan said, 'Sit down, Luke. I didn't figure you'd be back until morning.'

Smead was a short and stocky man, his hair and whiskers the color of dry prairie grass. His eyes were blue and penetrating. His was a singularly humorless face and his humorlessness was as much a part of him as his undeviating honesty. Dan knew he was going to have to evade, even if he didn't actually have to lie, and he hated it.

Smead asked, 'Who was the man that got shot tonight?'

Dan started to say he didn't know. Instead he shrugged without directly meeting the sheriff's eyes.

Smead asked, 'Wasn't there anything in his pockets to give us a lead?'

Dan suddenly remembered the things that had been in Hugh Wilkes's pockets. They were still in the side pocket of his coat where he had put them earlier. He took them out and laid them on the table.

Luke Smead gave everything but the wallet only a cursory glance. He picked up the wallet and looked at the thick sheaf of currency inside. Dan said, 'He was in the bank this afternoon according to Ned Winslow. Changed some gold into currency. A couple hundred dollars worth.'

He wished he'd had the foresight to go through the wallet down in the sheriff's office

14

earlier tonight. No telling what Luke Smead was going to find.

Smead counted the currency. There were two hundred and eleven dollars in all. He laid it on the table and began to go through the rest of the wallet, which was sweat-stained and worn. He found a few photographs, so worn and sweat-stained as to be almost unrecognizable. But Dan recognized one of them. It was a picture of Hugh Wilkes's wife, Loraleen.

Folded, and also sweat-stained, was a wanted poster with Sam Youngerman's picture on it. It must have been an old one because the reward, dead or alive, was only two thousand dollars. Smead spread the paper on the table and glanced up at Dan. 'What do you make of this?'

Dan said, 'Lots of people carry those just on the chance they'll run into him. Two thousand dollars is a lot of money, any way you look at it.'

'The reward's gone up to five thousand now.' Smead didn't seem to have noticed Dan's nervousness. He didn't seem to notice the tight, drawn look on Sarah's face. He was staring at the picture of Sam Youngerman. He said, 'There's something about this Youngerman. I keep thinking I've seen him someplace before.'

'You've probably seen him on a couple of dozen wanted posters in the last few years.'

'Yeah. I expect I have.' Smead gathered up

15

the dead man's effects. 'I'm going back to the office. I'll put these in the safe.'

'I should have done it. I guess having a killing in town made me forget. Shootings are kind of unusual in Dobeville.'

The sheriff smiled briefly at him. He went to the door, where he stopped and turned. 'You didn't see it, did you?'

Dan shook his head.

'Are you satisfied that Frank Delaney told the truth?'

Dan nodded. 'I walked past the saloon a couple of minutes before I heard the shots. Delaney was arguing with him. Plenty of people saw it and they all say Delaney was pushed into it. Besides, you know Frank. He wouldn't shoot anybody unless he was forced.'

'All right.' Smead went out and the screen door slammed. His boots thumped across the porch and scuffed down the gravel walk.

Dan crossed the room and closed the door. Sarah was looking at him, fright standing out in her eyes. 'You don't think he heard, do you Dan?'

'Heard us talking about Sam, you mean?'

She nodded.

He hadn't thought of that. But now he realized how voices carried on a summer night. Luke Smead might very well have heard them discussing Sam as he came up the walk. He might already have put two and two together. He might be trying to decide what he was

16

going to do.

Sarah was right, Dan thought. He had been stupid and stubborn in insisting on keeping his name. He could have changed it easily and then nothing like this would ever have come up.

But he hadn't changed it and now it was too late. Sam had located him through his name and through his official position as sheriff's deputy. That seemed fairly certain.

Sam would ruin him now because he hadn't changed his name. There didn't seem to be any way out. If he left now and Sam raided Dobeville, he'd be wanted right along with Sam and the rest of the Wilkes-Youngerman gang. If he stayed, and Sam raided the town, Dan might be lynched before the sheriff could intervene, or maybe in spite of his intervention on Dan's behalf.

But he still had a little time. Sam had to send someone else to scout the bank. He was too careful a man to raid a town that was strange to him.

Dan could only wait. And maybe pray.

CHAPTER THREE

Both Dan and his wife tossed sleeplessly far into the night. Even after Sarah began to breathe deeply and regularly, Dan remained awake, staring at the ceiling above the bed. He could hear the two children turning over occasionally in the other bedroom.

Tonight he was remembering a lot of things that had long been dead in his memory. He remembered the Quantrill raid on Lawrence, Kansas, in which he had taken part. Sam had been along on that raid. So had Silas Youngerman, and Lucas Wilkes, and Hugh. Other, younger members of both families who now belonged to the outlaw gang had not been old enough to participate.

Irregulars, Quantrill's band had been. Guerrillas. They had a list of names when they raided Lawrence. When they left, some of the names had been crossed off. The names had been those of hated abolitionists.

People since had accused Quantrill's men of looting and rape and even of killing children during the raid. Dan knew none of the stories had been true. There had been no looting, no raping. There had been no killing except for the men whose names were on the list and except for some who dared resist. Quantrill's men had set some fires before leaving, but the fires had been set in property belonging to men who were on the list.

After the Lawrence raid, Dan quit Quantrill's band and joined the regular Confederate cavalry. The other members of the Youngerman and Wilkes families had remained, but Dan hadn't wanted any more of making war on defenseless townspeople. If he

18

was going to fight, he wanted to fight soldiers like himself, who had the means and will to resist.

He turned his head and looked at Sarah's face. It was calm and peaceful now in sleep. Sarah had only been fifteen the year he rode away to join the regular army of the Confederacy, but even then Sam Youngerman had been in love with her.

Sam was six years older than his brother Dan and nine years older than Sarah. Frowning slightly now, Dan tried to remember Sam as he had been early in the war before bitterness changed him so. It was difficult to recall Sam's face without its heavy beard. But he'd always be able to recall Sam's eyes, blue and intense and almost fanatical sometimes. To Sam the war was a crusade, a holy cause. In his way he was as violent about it as the most violent of the abolitionists.

Only two things motivated Sam Youngerman's life during the four long years of war—his fanatical belief that he was fighting for a holy cause and his love for Sarah, who, when she was seventeen, would marry him.

Beside him, Sarah moved softly in her sleep. He wondered what she was dreaming. And he suddenly remembered coming home after the surrender at Appomattox Court House. He remembered the way she had looked at him when he saw her first.

Something had passed between them as

their eyes first met, something so powerful neither could have resisted it. Sam didn't matter any more. Nothing mattered but the two of them.

A wave of warmth and tenderness toward her flowed suddenly through his thoughts. Their courtship had been short. But he'd gone to Sam immediately after Sarah agreed to marry him. He'd told his older brother how things stood.

He could never forget the way Sam's face had looked. As cold as stone. And the eyes . . . they stared at Dan as if no bond of blood remained between the two. Dan remembered wondering if Sam was going to kill him then and there.

Suddenly aching in every tight-drawn muscle, Dan eased his legs over the side of the bed and sat up. He waited a moment before getting to his feet.

Silently, he crossed the room and went out into the hall. He went into the children's room and stared briefly at them, one after the other. Their faces, illuminated by the glow of moonlight outside the window, were peaceful and relaxed. Damn Sam anyway! He wouldn't care how much he hurt these two. He wouldn't even care if he ruined Sarah's life. Just so he got to Dan. Just so he revenged himself.

Revenge of one kind or another was all Sam had lived for since the war. He'd never accepted the fact that the war was ended, or that the South had suffered an overwhelming defeat.

So he went on raiding. And at last one day the occupation troops of the Union Army discovered where his hideout was.

It was the Wilkes family home deep in the wooded hills of western Arkansas. The troopers came on it when none of the menfolk were at home. There were only Ma Wilkes, and Grandma Wilkes, and two Wilkes girls, and a boy of ten whose name was Frankie. Also there had been Dan's mother and sister, Nellie, who were visiting.

In justice to the Union troopers, Dan had to admit that they probably hadn't even known no men were home. The women and the girls and young Frankie had fought as fiercely as if they had been men.

The end was predictable. Union Army gunfire coming from all sides and ripping into the cabin windows and doors finally killed the last of them. And when the commander of the patrol discovered what he had done, he had fired the cabin in a vain attempt to destroy the evidence.

The raid had given Sam the justification he needed for continuing his raids. Now he had something definite to avenge. And the raids became even more savage than they had been before.

Dan went silently down the stairs. He went through the kitchen and out onto the back

21

porch. He packed and lighted his pipe. Sitting on the back steps, he puffed it thoughtfully.

The moon was half-full. It put a soft, warm light on the trees and on the buildings of the town. He had been a fool for not changing his name. But he hadn't thought Sam's hatred would endure undiminished for seven years.

He heard the floor boards creak behind him and turned his head. Sarah stood there in the doorway, clad in her white nightgown. She said, 'Dan? Is there anything I can get for you?'

'No.'

'I guess I should have kept my promise and married him. Maybe if I had, he wouldn't be the way he is.'

He moved over on the step. 'Come and sit down.'

She obeyed silently and sat there close to him, shivering.

Dan said, 'Promising yourself to Sam before you were old enough to know your own mind was wrong. You know it and I know it and Sam knows it too. Sam's twisted, Sarah. He isn't right in the head. He kills and burns and steals and he tries to use the war to justify himself. He's my brother but he's a mad dog and you know he is.'

'What are you going to do if you discover that he's really going to raid the town?'

He puffed for a moment before he replied. 'Maybe I can keep him from coming here.

22

Maybe I can catch his spies when they show up.'

'What could you do with them? You couldn't throw them in jail without running the risk that they would talk.'

'They wouldn't talk. There's a price on the head of every one of them.' But he knew she was right. He couldn't risk throwing any members of the Wilkes-Youngerman gang in jail. Even if he had a charge to back up the arrests.

She was silent for a while. At last she asked puzzledly, 'Why is he like he is, Dan? What makes Sam so bitter and angry about everything? When I was a girl I looked up to him. He was like a god. I thought being his wife would be the most wonderful thing that could happen to me. I guess that's why I agreed to marry him.'

Dan shrugged. He didn't know what was really the matter with Sam. What he did know was that Sam couldn't stand to lose at anything. He hadn't attended the wedding when Sarah and Dan were married. He'd watched from the grove of trees across from the church. He'd watched and when Dan and Sarah drove past in their wagon . . .

Suddenly Dan's whole body felt cold. He admitted that he was afraid of Sam. He had always been afraid of the slumbering violence and savagery that he had sensed in his brother even when he had been a boy.

23

Sam had halted them as they drove past the grove of trees. He had stepped into the road in front of the team, forcing Dan to draw the horses to a halt. He had glowered at Dan for several minutes before he said, 'I can't kill you because you're blood kin to me. But I'll fix you for this. I'll fix you if it takes me the rest of my life.'

Dan had slapped the horses' backs with the reins. Sam had stepped out of the way and Dan had not looked around. But still sometimes he could feel the impact of Sam's hostile stare against his back.

Sarah had shivered continuously for more than an hour. And she'd had spells of quiet for days afterward when he knew she was thinking about Sam.

He got suddenly to his feet. He reached down a hand and when Sarah took it, pulled her up. For a moment he held her trembling body in his arms. Then he released her and followed her into the house.

He could reassure her but reassurance was meaningless. Both of them knew Sam was coming. Neither knew how they were going to cope with him. Sarah's hand suddenly gripped Dan's almost frantically as they climbed the darkened stairs.

*   *   *

Sarah eventually went to sleep, but Dan did

not. He lay wide awake all night, his mind flooded with memories of his boyhood—of the war—of the last seven years here in Dobeville.

They had been good years, the best of his life. There would be more good years ahead. Luke Smead was talking about retiring. If Smead threw his support to Dan, there was little doubt that he could be elected in Smead's place.

Now Sam was threatening all of that. Hugh Wilkes's presence in Dobeville had threatened it. Suddenly Dan began to sweat. What if someone recognized Hugh before they buried him? What if Luke Smead had overheard him talking to Sarah about Sam last night?

He got up when the sky turned gray and, carrying his clothes, tiptoed downstairs. He washed in the kitchen and shaved, then crammed on his hat and headed for the jail.

The morning air was cool and as he walked, the sun climbed out of the undulating eastern plain. He stared around him at the town, at the towering cottonwoods that lined its dusty streets, at the white picket fences and browning lawns, at the sturdy frame homes and business establishments. There was a future here for him and for his children too. Somehow he had to prevent Sam from bringing trouble to them all. Somehow he had to keep Sam's vengeful violence away.

The streets were deserted at this time of day, except for Hans Overstreet, who owned the saloon and who got up at dawn every day to come down and clean out the mess left over from the night before.

Overstreet angled across the street when he saw Dan and walked with him as far as the jail. He asked, 'Ever find out who that stranger was that got killed last night?'

Dan shook his head.

'Nothing in his pockets, eh?'

'Nothing with his name on it.'

'Southerner, likely, though. The way he was cussin' Grant.'

'I didn't know you were there.'

'I wasn't. Gib Duncan came by the house after he closed up. He said the stranger's horse was still tied out front when he went home. He took him down to the stable and put him in a stall.'

Dan wondered why he hadn't thought about Hugh's horse. Maybe he'd just assumed Hugh had stabled the horse when he hit town. Most people did.

Overstreet went on down and unlocked the saloon. Dan passed up the jail and went instead to the big, yellow frame livery stable. There was a big sign painted on the front of it. 'Dobeville Livery. Est. 1863. Rodney Dollar, Prop.'

He went in. It was cool and smelled of hay and dry manure, of horses and saddle leather. He walked along the line of stalls. Hugh's horse wasn't hard to spot. There was mud on

26

his legs and dry sweat on his neck. The saddle had been thrown up onto the partition between the stalls and the bridle had been hung on the saddle horn.

There were a pair of saddlebags hanging across the saddle. The initials H.W. were visible on the leather of the flap.

Dan opened them. There were some dirty clothes in one of them, some sack tobacco in the other one. There was a powder horn and a pouch of percussion caps beneath the dirty clothes.

Dan gave the horse a couple of forks of hay and went back out into the sun-washed street. Hugh Wilkes had not been a fool. There was a price on his head and he'd had better sense than to carry anything that could identify him.

Dan began to breathe easier, even though he knew he would not be completely safe until Hugh Wilkes was underground.

CHAPTER FOUR

The sheriff came into the office at eight. The sun was hot in the street, and there was a faint shine of perspiration on his balding head when he took off his hat and hung it on the coat tree just inside the door. The fringe of gray hair around his bald spot was damp. 'Going to be a scorcher,' he said.

He sat down at his desk and got out the pike of wanted posters from the drawer. He went through them deliberately and thoughtfully. Dan tried to remember if there had been any posters on Hugh Wilkes. He decided there had not. So far as he knew, there were no photographs of Hugh. That was probably why Sam had sent him here.

Finished, Smead returned the posters to the drawer and got up. 'I'm going over to Smitherman's and look at the corpse. Want to come along?'

Dan didn't particularly want to go but neither did he want to risk puzzling Smead by saying no. He nodded, got up, and put on his hat. He followed Smead out the door, pulling it closed behind him against the sun heat building up in the street.

Smead walked toward Smitherman's Furniture Store, a block up the street. Dan kept pace with him. Once, he glanced at the sheriff's face, wondering how much Smead had overheard last night.

They reached Smitherman's and Dan held the door for Smead, then followed him inside. There were a few pieces of furniture in the front of the store. Toward the rear, two styles of coffins were on display. On the left side of the back room was an area occupied by a couple of desks and some file cabinets, and by a room walled off from the rest by a partition about seven feet high. On the other side was

Smitherman's cabinetshop where he made his caskets and furniture.

Ian Smitherman was a stocky man with a canvas apron on. He wore muttonchop side whiskers but no beard. His 'eyes were a washed-out blue. He said in his British-accented voice, 'Come to see the corpse, Mr. Smead?'

Smead nodded, and gestured with his head toward the door in the partition. 'He's in there, I expect?'

'Yes, sir. Just go on in. You'd best plan on burying him today. It's going to be beastly hot.'

Smead nodded. 'You can plan the burial for this afternoon. Get the preacher to say a few words at the graveside, and let me know when it's going to be.'

'Aye.'

Smead opened the door and stepped into the room where the dead man lay. Dan followed. Smead pulled the sheet back and stared at Hugh Wilkes's face. It was very pale, by which fact Dan deduced that Wilkes had bled internally. Smead looked at it several moments. Then, with no visible sign of distaste, he opened the dead man's shirt and stared at his naked, hairy chest. He pulled up the dead man's sleeves and stared at his arms. He turned and glanced at Dan. 'Sometimes they have tattoos.'

Dan realized suddenly that the blood had drained out of his face. The sheriff was staring at him. He asked, 'Want to go outside? I didn't know a corpse affected you like this.'

Dan said, 'Maybe it's the heat. I didn't sleep too well last night.' He tried to smile but the smile was forced. 'I guess it kind of upset me to have a man killed while you were away.'

Smead's eyes seemed to probe his thoughts. 'All right, Dan. I've seen all I need to see anyway.'

Dan went out into the main part of the store and the sheriff followed him. Smead thanked Smitherman briefly and said, 'The county won't have to pay for this one, Ian. The man had several hundred dollars on him. But keep it reasonable. I'll have to hold the money in case any of the man's kin shows up.'

Smitherman said, 'Does twenty-five dollars sound reasonable?'

'That'll be fine. Bring me a bill so I'll have something to show the dead man's heirs.'

Outside in the street, Smead stopped in the shade of Smitherman's canvas awning and fished in his pocket for his pipe. Having filled it, he handed the sack to Dan. When both pipes were going, he peered at Dan through the blue clouds of smoke. 'When I came to your door last night you and Sarah were talking about a man named Sam? Anyone I know?'

Frantically, Dan tried to recall what he had been saying about Sam just before he had heard the sheriff's footsteps on the porch.

Sarah had said something to the effect that if Sam raided Dobeville the townspeople would never believe Dan hadn't been a part of it. She'd said they'd send him to prison. He'd replied that it looked like Sam would forget after seven years and just let them alone and Sarah had said, 'Not Sam. He never forgets anything.' It was then that Dan had heard Smead's footsteps on the porch.

Smead said, 'Dan? Is something the matter with you?'

Dan pulled himself together with difficulty. He shook his head. 'It's nothing I can't handle, Luke.'

There was a moment of silence from Smead. 'Is it Sarah, Dan? You having trouble with her? Is Sam . . .?'

Dan laughed nervously. 'No. It's nothing like that, Luke. If I can't work it out, I'll let you know. And thanks for offering to help.'

Smead studied him a moment more. Then he shrugged. 'Take the day off if you want to, Dan.'

'No. I think I ought to go to that man's funeral.' He knew he was a fool for saying that. He should have taken the day off and stayed away from the funeral. But he had ridden with Hugh Wilkes. He had once been Hugh Wilkes's friend. He was related by blood to the Wilkeses and in the Arkansas hill country a blood relationship was not easily dismissed.

Smead was no longer looking at him but

there was a light frown of puzzlement on his face. He said, 'All right, Dan, if that's what you want. You can go in my place and I won't have to go.'

Dan changed the subject. 'Did you get your papers served up north?'

Smead nodded. He glanced up at the sun. 'Let's get back to the office and out of this damn heat.'

Relieved, Dan followed him. Smead went into the office but Dan halted in the doorway, a sudden thought racked his brain. What if the gang was waiting someplace just outside of town for Hugh to come back and report? He said, 'I'll be back later, Luke. I just thought of something I ought to do.'

Smead nodded disinterestedly. Or was he just acting? Dan shook his head impatiently as he headed uptown toward home. Was he imagining things? Was he dreaming up trouble where trouble did not exist?

The thought of Sam and the rest of the gang, maybe within half a day's ride, had shaken him up considerably, and he knew it was something he would have to check out before his mind would know any peace.

He approached the house by way of the alley in back of it. He didn't want to see Sarah now and he didn't want to explain. He saw Danny and Mae playing in the back yard but he was able to slip into the stable without being seen. Once inside, he paused at the rain-spotted window and stared out briefly at the two of them.

Anger began to stir in him, anger at Sam and at the whole bunch of lawless Wilkeses and Youngermans. Saddling his horse, he led him out into the alley behind the house where he mounted and rode toward the livery barn. Wilkes's horse was stabled there.

He became determined that Sam wasn't going to succeed in raiding Dobeville's bank and ruining his life and Sarah's and the lives of their two little kids. Somehow he was going to stop Sam. He didn't know how right now, but he did know he would figure something out.

He reached the livery stable and dismounted just inside the big open doors. He walked to the stall where Wilkes's horse had been earlier. He went into the stall with the animal and lifted his feet, one after the other, studying each hoof carefully. At last, satisfied that he'd recognize the horse's tracks, he walked back to where he had left his own animal.

Rod Dollar, who owned the stable, met him as he was riding out into the street. He looked at Dan questioningly. Dan said, 'I was just looking at the dead man's horse. I think you might as well sell him if you get the chance. I can't see much sense in running up a big stable bill.'

Dollar, a tall, gaunt man of sixty, grinned ruefully. 'Whatever you say, Dan. I guess a

33

commission on selling the horse is better than nothing.'

Dan rode down the street. There were three roads coming into town and he intended to check all three for the tracks made by Hugh's horse yesterday.

Studying the dusty road carefully, he rode almost a mile out of town without finding any tracks that resembled those of Hugh Wilkes's horse. Satisfied that Hugh had not used this road, which came from the north, he cut across country toward the one that came into Dobeville from the east.

He intersected it about three quarters of a mile from town. He studied its dusty surface equally carefully. There had been a lot of traffic along this road both yesterday and today, but at last he found some horse's tracks at the side of the road where the rider had apparently pulled off to let a wagon pass. He dismounted, knelt, and peered closely at the tracks.

They were not too clear but he could tell that they were the tracks of the horse Wilkes had ridden into Dobeville. They had approached town from the east.

With his frown deepening, Dan remounted and headed east. He didn't know how far he was going to follow the horse's tracks. Not so far that he couldn't get back for the funeral this afternoon. But he had hoped to go far enough to find out one way or another whether

34

Hugh had come here alone, or whether the whole gang was waiting for him in some ravine within easy-striking distance of the town.

CHAPTER FIVE

It was not easy backtracking Wilkes. The road had been well traveled since Wilkes rode along it into Dobeville and only occasionally was Dan able to single out one of the tracks of Wilkes's horse.

He watched particularly along the sides of the road, not wanting to miss the place where Wilkes had entered it. It was slow going and the hours passed.

But at last Dan found the tracks of Wilkes's horse entering the road, and left it himself, backtracking still. He raised his head often, scanning the rolling hills ahead. The fact that Wilkes had come from this direction strengthened his suspicion that the whole gang was hiding out someplace nearby, and he didn't want to be spotted by any lookouts they might have stationed near their camp.

The trail stayed in the shallow draws winding through the sagebrush-covered hills. Dan began to grow increasingly uneasy as he continued to follow it.

He was a fool. Suppose someone from town was following him? Suppose they also found the camp of the outlaw gang? After that, he'd never be able to convince anyone he wasn't an active member of the gang. But why should anyone be following him?

He shook himself irritably as though to shake off his nervousness. In a clump of scrub cottonwoods, he reined his horse to a sudden halt. He was behaving stupidly. He knew the country hereabouts. Using his head would locate the outlaw camp sooner than blindly backtracking Wilkes. If the gang *was* camped nearby, he could find their camp easily enough. They would need water wherever they were and water was not exactly plentiful in these dry hills. There was, in fact, only one stream in the area and it was dry along most of its length. Only in three places did it rise out of the sand.

Grinning ruefully to himself, Dan headed for the nearest place where surface water was available in the creek. He'd have to stop letting his worry about the gang's presence in the area keep him from thinking as clearly as he should. He was going to need all his wits about him during the next few days.

Short of the spot by half a mile, he dismounted and tied his horse to a clump of brush. Afoot, he began working his way among the low-rounded hills. When but one ridge separated him from the place, he bellied down behind a clump of brush and carefully scanned the land ahead.

He saw no one. Aware that didn't mean no one was there, he began a cautious advance. He stayed in the bottom of the gully and moved slowly so as to attract no attention by quick and sudden movements.

This small gully emptied into the larger ravine that held the creek. Perhaps because there was more moisture here, the brush was thicker than it was elsewhere, and in the ravine that held the creek, there were willows and scrub cottonwoods. A blue haze seemed to hang above the creek. Suddenly Dan's body froze.

Smoke. The haze was one of campfire smoke, not dissipated by the breeze. He eased on ahead down the shallowing gully, hoping he could reach the trees and brush in the creek bed without being seen. The camp probably belonged to the gang but he wanted to be sure.

A clear space separated the end of the gully from the nearest brush and trees. Dan halted and stared back at the nearest slope. A slight movement near its top caught his eye.

There was a lookout there, sitting comfortably with his back against a rock. Dan watched a cloud of tobacco smoke drift away from the man. This was the movement that had caught his eye, this drift of tobacco smoke.

The man did not appear to be looking at him. Dan eased toward the creek, moving almost imperceptibly, crawling on his elbows and his knees. He kept his head turned, his eyes on the lounging lookout up above.

Seconds seemed to drag into hours. Once Dan froze as the lookout turned his head.

A sigh of relief escaped him when the lookout once more glanced the other way. Dan resumed his maddeningly deliberate crawl.

He reached the underbrush. He was covered with sweat from head to foot. His knees were trembling when he rose. He leaned against a tree for a moment to steady himself.

Carefully now, he moved upstream. The water that rose in the creek bed about half a mile above this place sank into it again less than two hundred yards from where Dan was right now. So the outlaw camp must be very close.

As he eased through the heavy underbrush, he glanced nervously up at the sun. He wanted to be back in time for Wilkes's funeral. He had promised Smead that he would attend as the sheriff's representative. But this was something that could not be rushed. If he was caught by the gang . . . He couldn't begin to guess what Sam would do. He did know he could be shot before Sam or the others even realized who he was.

Suddenly he stopped, turned motionless by a smell of campfire smoke. And almost at the same instant, he heard the faint sound of a man's deep voice.

Even more silently, more cautiously than before, he eased on ahead. And at last he caught a glimpse of the campfire from which the smoke cloud rose. He also saw a man cross between the fire and where he stood.

The distance was great, nearly four hundred yards. He squinted, trying to recognize the man.

He could not be sure he had never seen the man before. But suddenly into his view came another he could not fail to recognize.

It was Sam Youngerman. There was no mistaking that huge, broad-shouldered, deep-chested giant of a man. The beard was full, just as it had always been, making him look like a patriarch out of some long-dead period of the past. His long hair curled on his great, thick neck.

The day of the Lawrence, Kansas raid was suddenly vivid and fresh in Dan's memory because Sam was dressed almost exactly as he had been dressed that day—gray shirt and pants, floppy, broad-brimmed gray hat. Two pistols thrust into his belt. A rifle in his hands even though he was in camp. He never moved without that rifle in his hands. Dan remembered that.

Sam passed from his sight but Dan didn't immediately move. Old memories flooded through his mind—the good ones—the bad. Sam was his brother but also his mortal enemy. Yet how could he ever raise a hand against Sam Youngerman?

Another man passed into view down there,

and another still. Dan waited, scarcely daring to breathe. He had to know approximately how many there were. He had to know what the town of Dobeville was up against.

Others crossed the little open space between Dan and the gang's campfire. Some he recognized. Two were his brothers. Two more were cousins belonging to the Wilkes family. One was his uncle, Rufus Wilkes.

So far he had counted eight, but he had to assume there were more. It didn't make sense that they all would obligingly show themselves to him. He remembered the lookout on the hill. There must be another on the hill across the ravine. That would make ten for sure.

Ten men, at the very least, armed and exceedingly dangerous. Most of them had ridden with Quantrill's irregulars during the war, and afterward had fought pitched battles with the forces of the law. They were a match for three times their number of ordinary men. Perhaps that was why the very names, Youngerman and Wilkes, could inspire so much fear.

In the outlaw camp, Sam kept pacing nervously back and forth. Once he bawled something at someone beyond Dan's range of vision. Dan couldn't understand his words, but it was obvious that Sam was angry and irritable. Dan grinned faintly to himself. Sam knew Hugh Wilkes should have been back by now. He was irritable as he had always been when something unforeseen upset or delayed his plans.

Before moving, Dan turned his head and inspected every square yard of landscape within his range of vision. Then, more carefully than when he had advanced to this position originally, he began slowly to withdraw.

This, he thought ruefully to himself, was just like it had been during the war. You learned to scout silently or you died.

His mind racing, he eased out of the valley and back up the hill, toward his horse. He kept the lookout in view most of the time until he actually reached the shelter of the gully he had descended earlier, moving only when the lookout's gaze was directed the other way and even then, with great deliberation and cautiousness.

Once in the shelter of the gully, he stopped and dragged his bandanna from his pocket to mop the sweat and grime from his face. He looked at his hands and discovered they were trembling. What was he going to do? How could he prevent a raid on Dobeville when he didn't even dare tell the townspeople one was imminent? The minute he told them anything, they'd accuse him of being a part of it.

Rested, he raised his head cautiously above the lip of the shallow gully to check the lookout on the slope. He stiffened. His gaze roved back and forth anxiously but he did not see the man. The lookout had disappeared.

Something cold suddenly crawled along his spine. If the lookout had disappeared, it could mean but one thing. He had spotted Dan crawling up the slope. He was even now moving along an intercepting course.

Again Dan raised his head. This time his gaze was almost frantic as he searched the slope. But he still saw nothing and there was no sound.

He glanced behind him, looking for another route by which he could retreat and reach his horse. There was none. The slope lay exposed to the valley below. The only cover was provided by low clumps of brush. A man would have to crawl all the way if he tried to escape that way, and even so, he would, at times, be visible.

He didn't have that much time. He had to get out of here before the lookout intercepted him. A gunshot would bring the gang racing up the hill. Even a shout might be heard below.

Crouching, he ran up the gully, stumbling recklessly over rocks and low clumps of brush, sometimes falling in his frantic haste. If the man was planning to intercept him, it would not be this low on the slope. It would be higher up, so there was little use in being stealthy here.

He was panting heavily before he had gone three hundred yards. Sweat poured down both sides of his face. Near the crest of the ridge, where the gully widened, he stopped for breath.

He forced his breathing to quiet. His eyes searched both sides of the gully. Nothing moved. There was no sound. Yet the menace of the lookout's presence seemed thick and tangible.

What would the man expect of him? He would expect him to try reaching his horse as quickly as possible. The man might even have backtracked him all the way to his horse and be waiting there.

Then he would do the unexpected. He would try to find the lookout's trail. Then the hunted would become the hunter as he trailed the man.

Up here, the brush was higher than it had been on the slope. Crouched low, occasionally crawling or bellied down in grass, he made his way diagonally toward the top of the rounded ridge.

The trail was not hard to find. The grass was crushed from the man's running feet, and in places the ground was indented deeply by the lookout's boots.

Dan turned into it, raising up occasionally to stare ahead. He was now no more than a quarter mile from where he had left his horse. He was almost certain he would find the man waiting there for him.

He came to the place where the lookout's trail and his own merged and became one. Now he stopped, frowning, trying to decide

43

what he should do. Approaching from this direction, he had little chance of surprising the man. And unless he did surprise him, he would have to shoot, thus bringing the whole gang into it.

He'd have to circle then, and the wider he circled the more chance he'd have of reaching the opposite side of the man without being seen. Yet speed was important too. If he didn't show up in a reasonable time, the lookout might expect him from another direction.

Breathing slowly and regularly, he advanced at a crouching run, his eyes darting back and forth with all the wariness of a hunting animal.

CHAPTER SIX

The brush was almost high enough to conceal a running man, but Dan did not circle back toward the lookout until he was well past the place he had left his horse.

Having finally turned back, he stopped, listening carefully. He could faintly hear his horse stamping, could hear the bit jangling as the horse tossed his head, fighting off the flies.

With the horse located, Dan now advanced again, still crouching, his eyes intent. He was only thirty yards from his horse when he heard an unexpected sound close by.

He glanced that way and caught a flash of

movement through the heavy brush. He wondered if the man had also spotted him, but he didn't wait to see. As silently as possible, he moved toward the spot where he had caught that flash of movement only a split second before. He still held his gun ready in his hand even though he would not use it except as a last resort.

Again he caught the movement, now ahead of him and barely visible through the brush. This time it was identifiable as a man's back. Apparently, then, the man had not yet seen him nor heard him because of the noise he was making himself.

Dan followed, a sudden and disquieting thought passing through his mind. What would he do if the man ahead turned out to be one of his brothers? Or even one of his cousins? He thought he had seen all three of his brothers down at the outlaw's camp, but the distance had been great enough to allow for a mistake.

He put the thought resolutely from his mind. There was no time for doubt. The man ahead was a threat that had to be removed, if only temporarily. He didn't dare try for his horse with the man so close.

Traveling through this brush without making noise was next to impossible. So now he moved only when the man ahead of him moved, stopping instantly each time his quarry stopped.

This way he came to within a dozen yards of

the outlaw before he was heard. The man whirled and Dan saw immediately that the lookout was a stranger to him. He felt a rush of relief in spite of the moment's urgency.

The man's rifle was coming up, but Dan chose not to shoot. Instead he closed the distance between them with a long, low, running dive that threw him into the man's knees and brought the outlaw tumbling down on top of him.

The rifle had not discharged, and now the force of the impact tore it out of the outlaw's hands and flung it into a clump of brush a dozen feet away. The man cursed savagely.

Dan rolled, trying to break free, trying to hit the side of the man's head with his gun. He struck the outlaw's shoulder instead, and the blow brought another grunting curse from him.

The outlaw was fighting savagely, having overcome his surprise. His hand closed on Dan's gun and he tried frantically to wrench it away.

Dan kneed him in the groin and the pain brought another curse from him. Both of the man's hands were now occupied with trying to wrench Dan's gun away. Dan was glad the hammer had not been back. Had it been, the gun would most certainly have discharged.

He didn't dare lose the gun. He kneed the man again, then slammed an elbow straight to the man's throat with a short and savage jab. The man gagged and then began to choke.

Dan tore the gun away and brought it slamming against the side of his head.

The man fell back against the ground. He choked again. His face turned red, then blue, and then, surprisingly, his chest was still.

Dan stared unbelievingly. He hadn't thought he'd hit the outlaw hard enough to cause death, but apparently he had. Or else the blow had been enough to make the man's already labored breathing stop.

It didn't matter. The outlaw would have killed him if he could. What did matter was that sooner or later the gang was going to find the body of this man. They would also find Dan's tracks and the tracks of his horse.

He hurried toward his horse. He was still panting raggedly from the exertion of the fight. His hands and knees were trembling. His body was bathed with sweat. This was not the first time he had fought hand-to-hand combat for his life, and it probably wouldn't be the last. But it always affected him this way. He always trembled for an hour afterward. He always felt cold even though he was soaked with sweat.

He reached the horse and climbed wearily into the saddle. He turned toward town. There was grim satisfaction in him as he thought of the way Sam's face would look when he discovered his lookout dead. He could imagine the expression on Sam's face when they trailed the lookout's killer into the town of Dobeville.

Dan's horse picked his way down off the

brushy knoll. He followed the erratic course of the various shallow ravines winding between the rounded hills, until he reached the road.

Once on the road, Dan lifted the horse to a steady, rolling lope. It was already past noon and he supposed Hugh Wilkes's funeral would be at two. He had barely enough time to make it back to town.

But he had verified the presence of Sam Youngerman and the gang. And by verifying their presence, he had substantiated his suspicion that Sam intended to raid Dobeville.

He had also struck the first blow. Besides losing Hugh, they had now lost another man, the lookout on the hill. They soon would be aware that their presence in the area was known in Dobeville.

Knowing that, it was just possible that the gang members would refuse to go through with the raid. Reluctantly Dan shook his head. It was possible but it wasn't likely. Sam had too strong a grip on the members of the gang. They were all afraid of him.

He realized that he had spurred his horse into a reckless run. He saw the town in the distance ahead and slowed the horse to a steady trot.

The streets of Dobeville seemed crowded for this time of day. The funeral, he supposed. He entered town and rode down the dusty street toward the sheriff's office. Townspeople were clustered in small groups along the length of Main, talking among themselves. Dan looked at his watch. It was almost two.

He dismounted in front of the jail and looped his reins around the rail. He went inside, suddenly aware that his clothes were dusty from the fight out in the brush near the outlaw camp, dusty also from crawling along the ground trying to get close to it.

Smead was sitting at his desk. He looked at Dan, obviously not missing his dusty clothes. 'Where have you been? You look like you'd been in a fight.'

'Rattlesnake spooked my horse.' Dan tried to make his grin look shamefaced. 'I was thinking about something else and he dumped me.'

Smead seemed to accept the explanation although he looked a little puzzled. He was probably wondering what Dan had been doing outside of town.

Dan asked, 'What time's the funeral?'

'It was supposed to be at two. But John Temple came into town and went down to Smitherman's to look at the body. He recognized the man. He says he was in Lawrence when Quantrill raided it and he swears the dead man was one of Quantrill's men. He thinks his name was Wilkes. He heard someone call him Hugh.'

Dan glanced quickly at Smead, but the sheriff wasn't looking at him. Dan said, 'That raid was a long time ago. How can he be sure?'

'He isn't absolutely sure.' The sheriff glanced up at Dan. 'But he says he's pretty sure. Now suppose he's right. What do you suppose Hugh Wilkes was doing in Dobeville?'

Dan said, 'Wilkes is a member of the Youngerman gang, isn't he?'

'Ye. He's a cousin to the Youngerman brothers.'

Dan said, 'Maybe the gang's planning to raid Dobeville.' He held his breath after he said that, waiting to see what the sheriff's reaction was going to be. It might have been foolish of him to say it, but it had seemed like too good a chance to miss.

Smead only shook his head. 'I doubt it. We're several hundred miles from where they operate.'

'That doesn't mean . . .'

'I know it doesn't. And you're not the only one who's thought of the possibility. The whole town's buzzing.'

That explained the knots of people up and down the street, Dan thought. It explained the hushed way they were talking with each other. Maybe . . .

But he shook his head. It would take more than somebody's wild guess to really put the town on guard. Besides, even if they believed Wilkes had been here for the purpose of scouting the town, they'd have no way of guessing the raid would take place so soon. They'd be completely unprepared.

50

Dan said, 'I haven't had anything to eat. Will I have time to grab a bite before the funeral?'

Smead nodded. 'It'll be an hour at least.' He shook his head. 'I'll never understand people if I live to be a hundred. Now that they think the dead man was Wilkes, they all want to attend his funeral.'

'What about Frank Delaney? What does he think?'

'I haven't talked to him. But if I was Frank, I'd be getting scared. The Youngermans and the Wilkeses have a way of hunting down anybody who kills a member of their family.'

'If the man was Wilkes, there'll be a reward, won't there?'

Smead nodded. 'There's a thousand dollars on him. I checked on it.'

'Do you suppose Delaney knows about the reward?'

'If he doesn't, he sure will soon.'

'If he takes it, there'll be a record of his name, won't there?'

'Yep. The gang won't have any trouble finding him. Unless he takes the money and runs away.'

Dan went to the door. 'I'll be back in half an hour. I'm still planning to go to the funeral.'

Smead nodded absently but he didn't speak. He sat at his desk frowning at his thoughts. Dan realized the sheriff was considering the possibility that the gang might raid the town. He was trying to figure out what he ought to

51

do in case they did.

Dan untied his horse, mounted, and rode along the street toward home. Several people spoke to him. One man called, 'Hey Dan, did you hear who that dead man was?'

Dan nodded.

Another man yelled, 'He ought to know! His name's Youngerman!'

They all laughed and Dan forced himself to grin at them as if he also enjoyed the joke. He went on and turned the corner. His whole body was tense as a fiddle-string. What in the hell was he going to do? He owed the people of Dobeville a lot. Most of them were his friends. Even if nobody was hurt or killed when Sam raided the bank, they'd all be ruined financially. The bank would go broke and these people would lose everything they had.

He saw John Temple come out of the saddle shop. He stopped his horse and sat there looking down. The compulsion had been strong to avert his glance and go on without speaking to the man. He was glad he had successfully resisted it. He said, 'Hello, John.'

'Hello, Dan.' There was a slight frown on Temple's face as he stared up at Dan, as if he was trying to grasp some elusive thought or memory.

Dan said, 'The sheriff tells me you identified the dead man as Wilkes.'

Temple nodded, still frowning. 'I was in Lawrence when Quantrill made his raid.'

'Hasn't Wilkes changed quite a bit?'

'He's changed. But not so much I couldn't recognize him.'

'You're pretty sure, then, that it was Wilkes?'

'I'm damn near positive.'

Dan forced himself to grin. 'Frank Delaney should be glad to hear it. There's a thousand-dollar reward on Wilkes.' He nodded agreeably and went up the street, but he seemed to feel Temple's glance resting steadily on his back all the way.

CHAPTER SEVEN

The two children were taking their afternoon naps when Dan got home. Sarah came to the back door, a finger on her lips to warn him to be quiet as he came in. He went into the kitchen. Sarah stared at his dusty clothes with worried eyes. 'What happened, Dan?'

'Get me something to eat. I'll tell you while you do.'

She nodded and after a long, searching glance at him she began to prepare a meal.

Keeping his voice low so as not to wake the kids, Dan said, 'I backtracked Hugh. I found their camp. The whole gang is there.'

'How did you get so dusty?'

'Crawling up close. And fighting with one of

53

their guards.'

Her eyes were instantly concerned. 'Are you hurt?'

He shook his head. 'No. But I killed him. I didn't mean to but I did.'

Her face lost color. 'Who was he?'

'A stranger. And they have no way of knowing I'm the one who did it. But they won't have much trouble trailing me to town.'

'What are you going to do?'

He shrugged. 'I'll have to take things one at a time. Hugh has been identified. John Temple was in Lawrence when we raided it. He says he recognized Hugh.'

'Why hasn't he recognized you?'

'Maybe because he never got a good look at me at the time of the raid. But he's puzzled. I think he's bothered by the resemblance between Sam and me.'

'Do you think he'll make the connection?'

'Sure he will. Sooner or later.'

She continued to fix his dinner, frying bacon, scrambling eggs. Silently she put a plate in front of him and as silently he began to eat. Once she bent and kissed him lightly on the top of the head.

He finished as quickly as he could and then got up. 'I'll have to change for the funeral.'

He filled a washbasin and took it out onto the back porch to wash. Finished, he climbed the stairs quietly and put on a clean shirt, a tie, and his black Sunday suit. He hesitated a moment over the gun, then buckled it around his waist. He went back down the stairs.

Sarah was waiting in the kitchen for him. 'Do you want me to go to the funeral with you?'

He shook his head. 'I don't want to give anybody any more to talk about than they already have.'

'When will you be back?'

'I'll come home and change when it's over.'

'When do you think . . .?'

'Sam will probably send someone else to town, either tonight or early tomorrow. We don't have to worry about today.'

She nodded silently and he went outside. He mounted and rode back toward the center of town. He went up Main to Smitherman's because he wanted to know exactly when the burial was going to be. Frank Delaney was standing in front of Smitherman's store.

Dan looked down at him. 'I hear you're due to get a reward.'

Delaney glanced up worriedly. 'Not if they just up and bury him. John Temple says he's pretty sure he's Wilkes but that won't be good enough. I want some pictures taken of his face before they bury him.'

'What does the sheriff say?'

'He says it'll be all right. That's what I'm doing here now. Fedders is coming over to take the pictures.'

Dan started to leave, but halted again when

he saw Morgan Fedders coming, lugging his heavy camera. Dan dismounted and tied his horse, aware that Smitherman might refuse permission for the pictures to be taken unless he, as a representative of the sheriff's office, said it would be all right.

Delaney hurried to Fedders and took some of the photographic equipment from him. The two came on, talking between themselves.

Dan held the door, then followed them inside. They led the way back to the partitioned room where the body was. Smitherman appeared and Dan said, 'They're going to take some pictures of the dead man's face. Smead said it would be all right. They'll be needed for identification. There's a reward.'

Smitherman nodded, staring at Delaney. He turned to Dan as Delaney held the door for Fedders to go in. 'Does Frank know what that gang will do to him if they ever catch up with him?'

Delaney turned his head. 'What are you talking about?'

Smitherman said, 'That outfit sticks together. Anybody that does something to one of them answers to all the rest of them.'

Delaney said, 'It was self-defense. Everybody said so.'

'Do you think they'll care about a little thing like that? They . . .'

Dan said, 'Shut up, Smitherman. What the hell are you trying to do?'

56

'Tell him the truth. He'd better forget about that reward and get as far from Dobeville as he can. I sure as hell would if I was him.'

Delaney looked at Dan. Paler than before, he followed Fedders into the partitioned room where the body was. Dan turned and glanced at Smitherman. 'What time is the burial going to be?'

'Three o'clock. I've sent Jerry to the livery stable for the hearse. Looks like the whole town is going to turn out now that they know he was a member of the Wilkes-Youngerman gang.'

Dan didn't reply. There was a brilliant flash from behind the partition. He and Smitherman waited several minutes silently and at last there was another flash. Several minutes later there was a third. Smoke billowed across the ceiling.

Delaney came out. The alley doors of the store opened and Jerry Sandoval, who helped out in the store, came in, along with three other men. Outside in the alley, the black hearse gleamed. Sandoval said, 'We're ready, Mr. Smitherman.'

'All right. Take the casket out.'

Sandoval and the other three went into the little partitioned room where the body was. They came out, carrying the casket. They took it into the alley and loaded it in the hearse. Smitherman said, 'Drive slow through town so that anybody who wants to can follow you.'

Sandoval nodded. He closed the alley doors

57

behind him. Dan heard the wheels of the hearse grating on the gravel as it drove away.

He headed toward the front door. Frank Delaney followed him. Outside on the walk, Delaney asked anxiously, 'Dan, is what Smitherman said true? Will the Youngerman gang come after me?'

Dan nodded. 'They might.'

'What if I don't take the damn reward?'

'That's not going to make any difference.'

Delaney was silent, frowning worriedly for a long long time. His face was pale when he spoke again. 'What would you do if you was me?'

'I'd make myself scarce for a while. And I wouldn't let anyone know where I had gone.'

'But I haven't got any money. I'll have to wait until I get the reward.'

'I wouldn't wait.'

'How long is it going to take?'

'Two weeks to a month, I suppose.'

'Oh damn! Why should it take that long?'

'It just does. The people paying out that money have to be sure Wilkes is dead.'

'But . . .'

Dan said, 'You've got a horse. It doesn't take any money to get on him and ride.'

'I guess there ain't no big hurry. The gang can't find out that Wilkes is dead in less'n a couple of weeks.'

'Don't count on it. They could find out a lot sooner than you think.'

Dan untied his horse and swung to the animal's back. He reined around and headed down Main, a block behind the hearse. Already there were fifty or sixty people following it and the number was swelling all the time. Dan kept his distance, staying well behind the crowd.

There was only one reason for all the people going to the burial. Morbid curiosity. They knew the dead man was a member of the Wilkes-Youngerman gang. Dan wondered how long it would be before someone also connected him with the gang. Not long, now that no one was talking about anything else.

The hearse took the narrow two-track road that wound across the dry stream bed and up on the bluff where the cemetery was. By now the procession was more than a block long, but it was not a solemn one the way most funeral processions were. Nobody was grieving for the dead man. Everybody was talking, speculating about what Wilkes had been doing in Dobeville. Some said he'd been planning to rob the bank by himself. Others said the gang must have split up. Others thought he had just happened to be passing through. One man ventured the opinion that Wilkes might have been scouting the town so that the gang could raid the bank.

Charles Amherst, the Methodist minister, was waiting on the hill at the graveside. The hearse drove to the grave and Jerry Sandoval and the other three unloaded the coffin. They put it on ropes so that when the time came, they could lift it and lower it by means of the ropes.

The crowd gathered around the grave, forming a circle eight or ten deep. Dan remained on his horse a short distance away.

Amherst was a tall, gaunt, sad-looking man about sixty years old. He opened a Bible and read briefly from it in his solemn, sonorous voice. He nodded to Sandoval and he and the other three lowered the coffin into the grave. The minister stooped, picked up a handful of earth, and threw it into the grave. He said a short prayer, then closed the Bible in his hands. He turned away and began to walk back toward town.

Sandoval and another man began to fill in the grave. The crowd straggled away, following the minister. Dan urged his horse to a trot, and in a couple of minutes was well out ahead.

Sooner or later, he thought, every member of the gang was going to end up the way Hugh Wilkes had. That much was inevitable.

He rode past the bank, a red-brick building on the corner of Fourth and Main. The entrance was on a diagonal, facing directly into the intersection. The building had two stories. The second story was of wood with brown siding. It was occupied by Ralph Morris, an attorney, and by Doc Sinclair. There was a narrow balcony in front, but no doors opened onto the balcony, which was apparently only there for looks.

Dan knew he had to do something soon. Sam Youngerman was sure to send another member of the gang into town tonight. Things would move rapidly now, because Sam would know as soon as they found the dead lookout that someone had discovered their presence in the area. Sam was sure to guess that the unknown someone was his brother Dan.

He rode slowly home and tied his horse in back of the house. He went in and climbed the stairs to change his clothes. The children were playing in the upstairs bedroom and he stood in the doorway and grinned at them. The grin faded before the worry in his mind. He went into his and Sarah's room and swiftly changed his clothes.

His time was running out. He had to make up his mind what he was going to do. He had tonight, and perhaps tomorrow, and that was all.

CHAPTER EIGHT

The sheriff was gone when Dan got back to the jail. He went in, sat down, thoughtfully packed his pipe. He tried to imagine what Sam would do when he found the dead lookout.

He might come storming into town looking

for Dan but it wasn't probable. Sam had a temper and he wasn't afraid of anything but neither was he a fool. He had kept himself and the other members of the gang alive and at large by planning each job carefully.

Yet now that he knew his presence in the area was known, might he not give up the idea of raiding Dobeville? Dan shook his head. Sam had lost two men, one of them closely related to him by blood. He had not achieved the revenge for which he had come. No, Sam wasn't going to leave without making his raid.

He got up and crossed the room to the window. Moodily he stared into the street. The crowds were like those on Saturday, but nobody seemed to be getting anything done. They just stood around talking. Dan was willing to bet the saloons were full.

One reason Sam was so damned sure, he thought, was that he knew from experience how people were. He knew that law-abiding citizens are seldom able to get up enough courage to oppose organized lawlessness, particularly when that lawlessness is represented by a dozen bearded, heavily armed men whose reputations have preceded them. Sam figured the gang could handle any opposition the frightened townspeople might put up.

Smead came down the street and entered the jail. He nodded shortly at Dan, a slight frown of worry on his face. 'Well, I guess they got him buried all right. Did Fedders get the pictures before they did?'

Dan nodded. 'He took three. Frank Delaney wanted to know how long it would take to get the reward. I told him two weeks to a month.'

'That's about right.'

'Frank is scared and I can't blame him much. I told him he ought to get out of town.'

The sheriff glanced up. 'You really think that gang might be coming here?'

Dan said, 'We've got a bank, haven't we?'

There was a silence that lasted several moments. Facing the window, staring into the street, Dan said, 'Suppose you knew the gang *was* coming here to rob the bank. What would you do?'

'Deputize enough men to hold 'em off.'

'Do you really thing you'd be able to get men willing to fight off the Youngerman gang?'

'I think so. This is their town, as much as it is mine.'

Dan didn't reply. Smead asked curiously, 'What do you think the townspeople would do?'

Dan turned his head. 'Maybe I'm not giving them credit enough. But if it ever comes right down to it, you'd better close the bank before you tell the people the gang is coming. They'll make a run if you don't.'

'You don't give people much credit, do you?'

'Maybe not.'

'What would you suggest?'

Dan hesitated. He sensed that Smead was not just asking out of idle curiosity. He said, 'It would depend on how much time there was. If I could, I'd get troops from Fort Dodge. Otherwise, I suppose I'd have to do what you suggest—try to raise enough men in town to fight them off.'

Smead said, 'The trouble is, we won't have any advance warning. And I can't deputize men and keep them stationed around town indefinitely unless I've got more to go on than I have right now.'

Dan nodded hesitantly. Sam had ways of dealing with organized resistance. If a fusillade of bullets met him at the bank, he'd simply withdraw long enough to set fires at the edge of town, knowing the fires would immediately draw the defenders away from the bank.

The truth was, the town was at the mercy of Sam and his gang. Sam was going to loot its bank, kill some of its citizens, and leave it burning when he withdrew. It was going to be another Lawrence, only this time there would be no cause to justify the raid.

For one terrible moment, Dan considered riding to the outlaw camp and killing Sam himself. But he shook his head. He could never kill his own brother, no matter what Sam did or proposed to do. He couldn't kill Sam any more than Sam could kill him. That was the

64

awful part of it. The hatred between them had to be quenched with the blood of others.

The sheriff stood up suddenly. He said, 'Come on down to the saloon. I'll buy you a drink. Wilkes seems to have given us both the heebie-jeebies.'

Dan turned his head and grinned at Smead. The sheriff was a humorless, often dour man, but Dan liked him and always had. He said, 'That sounds like a good idea.'

Smead went out and Dan followed, pulling the door closed behind him. They walked side by side along the street toward the Free State Saloon.

The place was jammed, but the crowd made way for them. They reached the bar and Dan ordered beer. The sheriff followed suit. Gib Duncan, who was tending bar, slid brimming mugs along the bar to them.

A man shouted, 'Sheriff, what do you figure Wilkes was doing in Dobeville?'

Smead took a sip of beer before answering. Then he shrugged. 'Your guess is as good as mine.'

Someone else asked, 'You think the gang sent him to scout the town?'

Again the sheriff shrugged. The man persisted. 'What if they did?'

'Then I guess the gang will try and rob the bank. But don't forget, Wilkes never got out of town so the gang still doesn't have the information that they need. They'll have to send someone else.'

'Then we'd better watch out for strangers.'

Someone in the back of the room yelled, 'Especially if their name is Youngerman or Wilkes.'

Everybody laughed, most of them looking straight at Dan. For some reason, he had trouble meeting the eyes of those around him and his grin was strained and forced. He felt the sheriff watching and forced himself to look up. Smead's eyes met his and held for a long moment that seemed like an eternity. It was Dan who looked away.

The babble of voices went on. Dan finished his beer without enjoying it, and the sheriff did the same. Dan offered to buy another but Smead refused. They waited a moment there at the bar uneasily and at last Smead said bluntly, 'Let's go back to the office, Dan. I want to talk to you.'

Dan nodded. He followed the sheriff through the crowded room to the doors and out into the street. In silence they walked to the sheriff's office, Smead grimly, Dan uneasily.

Desperately he wanted to end the pretense. He wanted to confide in the sheriff, wanted to tell Smead who he really was. He wanted to tell where he had been this afternoon—that the whole Wilkes-Youngerman gang was waiting within a dozen miles of town.

He wanted to, but he knew that he would

not. Seven years of his life were here in Dobeville. He'd held this deputy's job most of that time. What could he do if the sheriff fired him? Nobody else would give him a job afterward. He'd simply have to leave, taking his family along with him. And if he did, Sam would have won.

Besides, Sam would come now whether Dan was here or not. Hugh had been killed in Dobeville. Another gang member had been killed out near the outlaw camp.

Smead opened the door and went inside. Dan followed and the sheriff closed the door. He said, 'I never asked you many questions when you came to work for me.'

Dan said, 'I know you didn't.'

'Maybe it's time I did.'

Dan forced himself to meet Smead's glance steadily. He asked bluntly, 'Why?'

'Because your name's Youngerman. Maybe some people can joke about the Youngerman gang raiding Dobeville, but it doesn't seem very funny to me.'

'You think I'm a member of the Youngerman family? You think there's a connection between me and that outlaw gang?'

'I didn't say that. But I want some questions answered and I want them answered now. I don't know what you're worried about if you've got nothing to hide.'

'Worried? Who said I was worried? Ask away.'

'All right. Where were you during the war?'

'Fighting for the South. What's wrong with that?'

'Dan, I'm sorry. I've got to ask. There's no use in us getting mad.'

Dan shrugged. He gave the name of his unit and the name of his commanding officer. He told Smead what his rank had been, both at the beginning of the war and at its end.

'Where were you born?'

Dan hesitated. So far, he had only evaded and had told no outright lies. But now he must, if he was going to avoid telling the sheriff everything. He said, 'Georgia. Near Atlanta.'

'Is that where you were raised?'

Dan nodded.

'I'd have said you talked more like Missouri or Arkansas.'

Dan said, 'I was born in Georgia. I can't help the way I talk. There were a lot of men from Missouri and Arkansas in my regiment.'

'Do you have any brothers or sisters?'

Dan frowned. This was like an inquisition, but he knew he was going to have to put up with it. He said, 'Two sisters and three brothers. They all live in Georgia.'

'How come you never get any mail from there? And how come you never write?'

Dan stared at the sheriff's face. Smead had guessed the truth, he realized. Smead knew he was related to Sam Youngerman and to the other members of the gang. He hadn't fooled

68

Smead for a minute but he had to go on with the pretense. Because Smead wouldn't act unless he had proof. He said, 'We never got along.'

'Who's the Sam you and Sarah were talking about the other night?'

'An old flame of Sarah's. When we haven't got anything better to argue about, we argue about him.' There was an edge in Dan's voice suddenly. He was beginning to resent Smead's distrust. After seven years of faithful law enforcement, a man was entitled to be trusted if he was entitled to nothing else.

Smead said, 'All right, Dan. I'm sorry for all the questions. But I had to know.'

The two stared at each other warily. Smead knew who he really was, Dan thought. Each of them knew exactly where the other stood, even though neither was saying so. He suddenly felt as if he was sitting on an open keg of powder, smoking a cigar.

CHAPTER NINE

Smead left early to go home for supper and Dan stayed, even though there was no real reason why he should. He hated to leave the central part of town. He hated to be where he could not keep his eye on the bank. Sam Youngerman was certain to send someone else in to scout the town and Dan didn't want to be away when he did.

The bank closed as usual at five, but Dan stayed until almost six. Then, regretfully, he locked the door of the sheriff's office and untied his horse, which had stood patiently outside at the rail most of the afternoon.

He swung to the horse's back, looked up and down the street once more, then turned toward home. He put the horse into the stable behind the house, unsaddled, and threw down some hay.

Both children were in the yard. They came running to him and he knelt and scooped them up in his arms. They were warm and soft and their arms went tight around his neck. Damn Sam. What right had he to come here after seven years and ruin the lives of Sarah and these two children and himself?

He put the children down and walked toward the back door, with the two running excitedly at his heels. The smell of frying meat came from the door. Sarah glanced up and smiled at him, her eyes worried and concerned, silently asking him if anything else had happened this afternoon. He said, 'It's all quiet so far. I doubt if anything is going to happen until tomorrow but I'm going downtown after supper anyway.'

She said, 'Get washed for supper, children,' and Dan helped them get washpans filled with water and then watched them, smiling, as they

70

washed. He washed his own hands, dried them, then followed the children to the table.

The meal was mostly silent, even though both Dan and Sarah tried to keep the children from knowing anything was wrong. As soon as it was over with, Dan got up, shot Sarah a look, and said, 'Get to bed early, kids. I'll see you tomorrow.' He knelt and accepted a hug and kiss from each of them, then went out the back door and walked toward the center of town.

Thinking of the children and of Sarah, he made himself a grim promise. Before he would let their lives be ruined, he would kill Sam. Even if Sam was his brother, he would kill him. But even as he made the promise, he knew deep inside himself that it could not be kept.

The street was quiet when he reached the corner of Fourth and Main. He stopped diagonally across from the bank and stared moodily at it. The bank hadn't been built to withstand the onslaught of a gang of bank robbers. The small side and rear windows were barred but the larger front windows were not. The door was just an ordinary door. Any kind of battering ram would break it down.

The bank's cash was kept in a tall, old-fashioned safe behind the barred grilles that faced the white-tiled lobby in the front. Dan had little doubt but that Sam had someone with him who could make short work of it. The Wilkes-Youngerman gang had been blowing safes for years, in banks, in railroad express

71

cars, even in courthouses. This safe wouldn't even slow them down.

If they were to be stopped, it would either have to be before they rode into town, or afterward—before they hit the bank. Provided enough men could be found with the courage to face them in a showdown fight.

Dan knew he couldn't stop them by himself unless he stopped them by killing Sam, and that was a way he could not force himself to take. He might be able to kill Sam in the actual defense of his life, or of the lives of Sarah and the kids. But not in any other way.

Sam knew it too, he thought sourly. Sam knew it and was depending on it.

The Free State Saloon was almost deserted at this time of day. Everybody was at home, eating supper. Only Frank Delaney and Gib Duncan were in the place.

Dan walked to the bar and stood beside Delaney. He nodded at Duncan and said, 'Beer, Gib.'

Gib Duncan drew the beer. Dan turned to Delaney. 'What did you decide to do?'

Delaney was a little drunk. His eyes were bloodshot and his mouth was slack. 'I'm going. I'm going to get out of town tonight. I guess I'll have to give up my job, but I'll write you where I'll be so you can send the money on to me.'

'What are you going to do with it? Buy yourself a ranch?'

'Uh huh. A thousand dollars will buy a pretty good piece of land and a few cattle too.'

Dan drank his beer. He kept thinking that if Sam *was* going to pull off a raid, the supper hour would be a mighty good time for it. He went outside and stared up and down the street. He walked down to the depot and looked around, then retraced his steps to the sheriff's office. Maybe if he told Smead everything, there would still be time to get troops here from Fort Dodge. A telegram could reach the commandant tonight. If he put troops on the train in the morning, they could be here by late tomorrow night. Provided, of course, that the Fort Dodge commandant didn't have to wire Washington or Omaha for authority.

Dan lighted a lamp in the office and sank down in the swivel chair. He tilted back, packed and lighted his pipe. He stared at his hands as they held the match. They were trembling.

Damn! If he tried to save the town and the bank, he would at the same time ruin his own life and the lives of his family. It was a hell of a choice for a man to have to make.

But if he could keep intercepting Sam's men as they came in to look the bank over, Sam might get discouraged and give it up. The members of the gang might get nervous if they kept losing men. They might refuse to go through with it.

He got up and walked to the window. Down at the lower end of town, a lone horseman was riding in. Dan couldn't recognize him at this distance and in this light.

Swiftly he returned to his desk and blew out the lamp. He crossed to the door and went outside.

The man had reached the livery stable and was turning in. Dan glanced up and down the street, then broke into a run as he crossed the street and headed for the livery barn. As he ran, he loosened his gun in its holster. He was glad no one was in the street and he knew the livery stable would be as deserted as the street. He could get rid of the newcomer if he had to and nobody would even know.

At the corner of the tall frame building he stopped, listening. He heard horses stamping inside the stable. He heard a man's deep voice speaking to his horse, but he could not make out any of the words.

He eased toward the big double doors opening into the street. He thought about drawing his gun, then decided against it. He didn't want to be seen creeping toward the stable doors with a gun in his hand.

He reached the doors and peered inside. He could see the vague shape of a man about halfway down the passageway leading the length of it from front to back. The man was putting his horse into one of the empty stalls.

Silently, Dan stepped through the doors,

74

immediately shifting to one side so that he would not be silhouetted against the gray light outside in the street. With the wall at his back, with the deep, dry manure on the floor underfoot, he called, 'Hold it, mister. Hold it right there.'

The man froze in the act of hanging his saddle on the partition between two stalls. Dan said, 'Go ahead. Put it up. Then turn around.'

The man carefully hung his saddle on the partition. He turned slowly around, his hands held stiffly away from his sides.

The light was bad and Dan could scarcely see the man. He realized that he had stopped here and called to the stranger, in preference to working his way closer, in the hope that the man would turn around shooting and thus give him a chance to return the fire and kill him. The stranger stood there tensely and Dan walked slowly toward him, careful not to get directly between him and the open doors.

He stopped a dozen yards away. He still hoped the stranger was going to draw. He said harshly, 'Who are you and what are you doing here?'

'Well now, do you always treat newcomers like this? I just rode in. I'm putting my horse up for the night, and when that's done I'm going to the hotel and get a bath. After that, I'm going to eat supper, and after that I'm going to have a drink or two. Then I'm going to go to bed.'

'Don't get smart. What's your name?'

'Will. Will Hawkins.'

'What did Sam tell you to find out?'

For the barest instant, Dan could see the tension that suddenly came into the man. Then he visibly relaxed. 'Sam? Who's Sam?'

Dan said, 'Turn around. Put your hands on the top of that partition between the stalls.'

Hawkins did as he was told. Dan stepped up carefully behind him and slid the gun out of the holster at Hawkins' side. He tossed it into the manure and straw on the floor, about twenty feet away.

'Now. Turn around and talk.'

'About what?'

'About Sam Youngerman. Or you'll be as dead as that lookout up on the hill above your camp.'

'So you're . . .?' The man stopped suddenly.

Dan nodded. 'I'm the one. And you've given yourself away.'

The man turned his head and stared over his shoulder at Dan. 'You don't need me to tell you anything. You know why Sam is here. He's going to clean out your tank-town bank. And you'll keep your mouth shut about it, because any of us that get caught will swear you're one of us and that you set up the robbery.'

Dan was silent. The man's story came as no news to him, yet it was a shock to hear it put into words by someone else. He said, 'What makes you think I won't just kill you now?'

'You won't. Because I won't draw on you, or put up a fight, and you couldn't kill me unless I did.'

Dan slapped him savagely on the side of the face. Even in the dim light inside the stable, he could see the way Hawkins' eyes narrowed, the way his mouth tightened with his sudden rage. Dan said, 'Maybe you'll change your mind.' He left the man and crossed to where he had thrown Hawkins' gun. He picked it up, brushed it off, then walked back and replaced it in the holster at Hawkins' side. He stepped back and said, 'You can put your hands down now.'

Hawkins turned but he did not lower his hands. Dan said, 'Pull it or I'll shoot you down and say you did!'

Eyes blazing, Hawkins nevertheless grinned steadily at him. Dan felt the frustration of helpless rage. He said, 'I could throw you in jail.'

'What for? I haven't done anything.'

Dan said, 'All right, then saddle up that horse and get out of town.'

Hawkins shook his head. Dan moved in close to him and deliberately hit him on the side of the face with the raking barrel of his gun. Hawkins staggered and blood rushed to the long gash. It ran down his cheek and collected on his jaw, to begin dripping steadily to the floor. Dan said harshly, 'I won't say it again.'

77

Hawkins put up a hand and touched the side of his face. He took the hand away and stared at it. He wiped it on his pants.

Turning, he removed his saddle from the partition and tossed it into place onto the back of his horse where the saddle blanket still remained. He cinched it down, then backed the horse out of the stall. He started to open his mouth but Dan said sourly, 'Never mind. I know what you're going to say—that you'll kill me for this. Better take it up with Sam. I don't think he wants me killed.'

Hawkins swung to his horse's back. He dug his spurred heels savagely into the horse's sides. The horse thundered out of the stable and into the street. By the time Dan reached the doors, horse and rider were out of sight.

CHAPTER TEN

Dan did not tell Sarah about Hawkins. He was ashamed of his own brutality toward the man. He could excuse himself on the grounds that he was fighting for his life and for the lives of his family, but he could not help feeling guilty and ashamed. He didn't want Sarah to know what he had done to force Hawkins to leave town.

He lay awake long after Sarah had gone to sleep, staring into the darkness, wondering

78

what he was going to do, and wondering what Sam would do next. He was almost sure that another member of the gang would be in tomorrow to scout the bank. Unless Hawkins had seen enough to give Sam the layout of the town.

The sky was growing light in the east when he finally went to sleep, and Sarah did not awaken him until his breakfast was ready in the morning. He washed his face hastily and sat down at the table, grinning ruefully at her. She said, 'I heard you tossing around most of the night and I hated to wake you up this morning.'

'I thought you were asleep.'

'I was, most of the time.'

He didn't feel like eating but he knew he'd feel better if he did. He gulped two cups of coffee with his breakfast, then excused himself and went out on the porch to shave. The children were still asleep when he left the house. Sarah didn't question him or ask him what he was going to do. She realized that he wouldn't know until he knew what Sam was going to do.

It was almost eight when Dan turned into Main. He recognized the woman as soon as he saw her standing there in front of the bank.

She was Jennie Wilkes, Hugh's older sister and the only female member of the gang. She was scrawny and dried up, but she was as tough as any man Dan had ever known. She could shoot as straight as any other member of the gang and if there was gentleness or womanliness in her, she had always managed to keep it from being visible.

She stared with open mockery at Dan. He turned his horse and rode to her, after first glancing up and down the street to see if anyone was watching him. There were maybe half a dozen people in the street, but none of them seemed to be paying attention to him or to the woman standing in front of the bank.

Inwardly he cursed Sam as he approached. Sam knew he wouldn't be able to treat Jennie the way he had treated Hawkins yesterday. Jennie could come into town and get out again without any trouble from Dan.

He stared down at her angrily. 'Hello, Jennie. It's been a long time, hasn't it?'

She nodded but she didn't speak.

'Have you found out what Sam wants to know?'

She gestured toward the bank with a toss of her head. 'I don't know why he needed to know anything. If the safe is anything like the bank, he can get into it with a can opener.'

'First you've got to get into the bank.'

'And who's going to stop us? You?'

'Maybe.' He continued to stare down at her, frowning. She was dressed in a man's clothes, gray woolen trousers, and gray shirt. She wore a floppy, cavalry style hat that was obviously too big for her. The only feminine article of apparel visible were her black high-button shoes. Her hair, graying and stringy, was tucked up into her hat. Only a few wisps escaped.

Her skin was like parchment and deeply tanned. It looked as if it might crack if she so much as smiled.

Dan said, 'Sam's almighty sure, isn't he? How does he know I won't be waiting for him with fifty guns when he rides in?'

'You're his brother. The blood tie is as strong in you as it is in him.'

'He'd better not count on it. Sarah and I have two little kids. I'm not going to stand by and see their lives ruined just so Sam can have his revenge.'

'Then get out of town.'

'He'd like that, wouldn't he? He'd like to make me a fugitive like he and the rest of my brothers are.'

She didn't answer that. She just stared up at him, her eyes smoldering. 'Where's the man that shot Hugh?'

'He's gone. He left town last night.'

'What's his name?'

Dan stared at her unbelievingly. 'You don't think I'd tell you, do you? I know what you'd do to him. You'd shoot him in the back, or you'd force a fight with him knowing all the time that he wouldn't draw on a woman no matter what she did.'

'What's his name?'

Dan shook his head. 'Get out of town, Jennie. I could throw you in jail you know.'

'And what would you charge me with?'

Dan didn't reply. He couldn't throw her in jail. She wouldn't hesitate to expose him if he did, even if by so doing she exposed herself. Sam would break her out of jail when he came in to raid the bank.

She asked mockingly, 'Are you through with me?'

He nodded.

'Then I'll be going. I want to ask around about the man who shot Hugh. I want to know where he's gone.'

Dan watched her go. She was small and scrawny and getting old but she walked like a cat. Somewhere on her was a gun, he knew, and wherever it was, she'd be able to get it out mighty fast.

She went into the Kansas Hotel and Dan rode down the street to the Free State Saloon. Hans Overstreet was sweeping the boardwalk in front of the place.

Without dismounting, Dan asked, 'Did Frank Delaney leave town last night?'

Overstreet stopped sweeping and leaned on his broom. He glanced up at Dan. 'I don't know how the hell he could. He had to be carried out of here. Far as I know, he's still over at the hotel.'

'What time was that?'

'When we closed. About one o'clock, I

suppose.'

Dan nodded. Frank was probably still asleep. Most likely he'd sleep until noon if he'd been drunk enough to pass out last night. So he was safe from Jennie for a while. She'd leave town before noon anyway.

He rode to the office and unlocked the door. He left his horse tied in front, knowing he might need the animal at any time.

He got a broom and began to sweep, glad of something to do. Every now and then he walked to the front door and peered into the street. Each time he looked across at the veranda and front door of the hotel, wondering why Jennie had not come out.

He wished Delaney had stayed sober last night. He wished he'd had the good sense to get out of town. But Delaney had stayed in town. He'd probably still be here when Sam and the gang came riding in.

He caught himself listening for the sound of gunshots from the direction of the hotel. He was almost ready to go there and see what was going on when he saw Jennie emerge into the morning sun.

She glanced toward the jail. Then she walked to the bank, where her horse was tied. She mounted and rode down the street to the Free State Saloon.

Dan began to pace nervously back and forth. Overstreet was going to be startled to have Jennie walk in and order whisky just like a man. He would probably be equally startled to have her express interest in the man who had shot Hugh Wilkes.

Gib Duncan came down the street and went into the saloon. He was there only a few minutes. When he emerged, he hurried straight toward the jail.

He was sweating when he came in. 'Dan, there's this woman down at the saloon. She's asking questions about Wilkes and Mr. Overstreet thinks she might be his wife or something. She wants to know who shot Wilkes.'

'Has he told her?'

'Huh uh.'

'All right, Gib. Thanks for telling me.'

'Hadn't you ought to arrest her or something?'

'For what? Asking questions?'

'Maybe she's a member of that Wilkes-Youngerman gang.'

'A woman? I doubt that, Gib.'

Gib looked at him puzzledly for a moment. 'What do you want me to tell Mr. Overstreet?'

'Tell him not to tell her anything. I'm trying to get Frank Delaney to leave town.'

'All right.' Gib hesitated another moment, then turned and went out into the street.

Dan stepped out of the office and closed the door. He hurried across toward the hotel. Before he went in, he glanced down at the saloon. Jennie was apparently still inside.

He went into the hotel and crossed to the desk. 'What room does Frank have?'

'Seven.' Larry Widemeier grinned. 'Man, he sure was drunk. They had to carry him upstairs.'

'You haven't seen him this morning, have you?'

'Huh uh. Funny thing, though. There was an old woman in here a while ago. She was asking if I knew anything about the man that shot Hugh Wilkes.'

'What'd you tell her?'

'I told her to see you. I figured she might be related to this Wilkes. Why else would she be asking questions like that? Did she come to see you?'

'I saw her.'

'Know who she is?'

Dan shrugged. 'She wouldn't say. Probably Wilkes's woman friend. Maybe she was traveling with him and when he didn't come back to where they were camped, she came looking for him. She looks like a rough one. I figured Frank ought to know she was in town.'

'Maybe you ought to throw her in the jug. She might be a member of that gang.'

'I haven't got any proof of that. And you can't just throw people in jail without a reason.'

'No. I guess you can't.'

Dan crossed the white-tiled lobby floor to the stairs. He climbed them heavily. At a door with a seven on it, he stopped and knocked.

For a long time there was no response. He pounded more heavily on the door. Down the hall, a woman's voice, muffled by the intervening wall and door, protested plaintively.

At last he heard a groan behind Delaney's door and the creaking of the bed. He heard someone fumbling with the door lock. A moment later the door opened.

Frank was still in his clothes, which were mussed and wrinkled from sleeping in them. His eyes were bloodshot. His face was unshaven and his mouth was slack. 'What the hell do *you* want? What's the idea, wakin' me up like this?'

Dan pushed past him and went into the room. He said, 'Shut the door and quit bellyaching. I thought I told you to get out of town.'

'I don't have to do what you tell me to.'

Dan stared at him disgustedly. He said, 'There's a rough-looking woman in town asking questions about the man that killed Hugh Wilkes. She's probably his woman friend or his wife and she looks capable of shooting you.'

'A woman? Hell I ain't going to let no woman run me out of town.'

'What would you do if she pulled a gun and started shooting at you?'

'I'd . . .' Delaney stopped, frowning.

Dan nodded. 'That's right. You wouldn't do

anything until it was too late because she's a woman. Besides that, you don't know but what there are more members of that damn gang camped right outside of town. If I was you, I'd get myself a drink and get the hell out of here. I wouldn't stop until I'd put fifty miles between me and Dobeville.'

Delaney was still frowning, but he nodded reluctantly. 'I guess you're right. Where's this woman now?'

'Down at the Free State. Go out the back door of the hotel. I'll get your horse and meet you there.'

'I could sure use a drink.'

'There's a little bit in a bottle down at the sheriff's office. I'll bring it along.'

He went out and down the stairs. He went into the bright sunlight in the street. It was already getting hot but there was a strange kind of chill in Dan, a chill the sun's heat could not drive away. Maybe he could save Frank's life by getting him out of town. But how was he going to save his own?

CHAPTER ELEVEN

Dan went back to the office first and got the pint bottle of whisky out of the desk drawer. Sticking it down into his hip pocket, he headed for the livery barn.

87

Rod Dollar was there. He brought Frank Delaney's horse out and saddled him. Dan said, 'Frank's got a big head this morning so I told him I'd bring him his horse and a drink. Just don't tell anybody about it. I wouldn't want anybody to know where Frank's gone or even when he left.'

'All right.'

Dan mounted Frank's horse and went out the back door. He took the alley uptown and stopped at the back door of the hotel.

Delaney was sitting in the dirt, his back against the hotel wall. His head was down on his folded arms, but he looked up as Dan approached. He said, 'God, what a head! Never again. I'm never going to take another drink.'

Dan handed him the bottle as he swung down off the horse. 'After this you can quit,' he said. 'Go on, drink it. If you can keep it down, it'll make you feel well enough to travel.'

Delaney shuddered as he put the bottle to his mouth. He drank, and coughed, then drank again. His face was grayish color and he had begun to sweat. Dan hoped he could keep the liquor down. If he didn't, he sure as hell wouldn't get far today.

Delaney started to put the bottle to his mouth again but Dan said, 'Wait a minute. See if what you've already taken stays down all right.'

Delaney went to his horse and put his head

down in his folded arms on the saddle. He stood that way for what seemed a long time. But when he raised his head again, there was a healthier color to his face. He said, 'I feel better Dan. I guess I'll get the hell out of here.'

Dan said, 'Don't go back to the ranch. And use the alley getting out of town.'

Delaney nodded. He mounted and turned his horse down the alley toward the depot at the lower end of town.

Dan waited until he was out of sight. Then, using the passageway beside the hotel, he returned to Main Street and walked across it to the jail.

He was facing a truth he should have faced yesterday. He could fool himself no longer. He had to tell Luke Smead who he was. He had to tell the sheriff that the whole Wilkes-Youngerman gang was less than a dozen miles from town and might raid it at any time. Sam was counting on his fear and his family loyalty to keep him silent, but Sam didn't know what seven years in a place could do for a man. He had no conception of the ties he forms living seven years in one place. Smead was in the office when Don arrived. Pulling the door shut behind him Dan said, 'I've got to talk to you.'

Smead glanced up. Dan said, 'I can't keep still about it any more. I'm Sam Youngerman's brother. The gang is waiting less than a dozen miles from town. They're going to raid the bank.'

89

Smead wasn't surprised, but Dan thought his face lost color. The sheriff asked, 'When?'

Dan shrugged. 'I don't know. Hugh Wilkes was here to scout the layout of the town. When Delaney killed him, Sam had to send another man. I caught him and pistol-whipped him down at the stable yesterday, and made him get out of town. But this morning there's another one. Jennie Wilkes. She's Hugh's sister and besides looking the bank over, she's been asking around town about Frank Delaney.'

'Where is she now?'

'Still down at the saloon, I guess.'

'Go pick her up. We'll put her in jail. That will be one less we'll have to face when they raid the bank.'

Dan nodded. He hesitated a moment, then asked, 'What are you going to do about me?'

Smead stared puzzledly at him. 'I don't know. I don't know what the pressure will be from the townspeople.'

'You've known me for seven years.'

Smead said, 'Go get this Jennie Wilkes. We'll talk about it when you get back.'

Dan went out. He strode swiftly down the street toward the saloon. He went inside.

Jennie Wilkes was at the bar, a bottle and glass in front of her. She turned her head and looked at Dan, a mocking expression in her eyes. It faded when Dan drew his gun. He said, 'Put your hands on the bar, Jennie, and keep

90

them there. The fact that you're a woman isn't going to mean a damn thing to me.'

For an instant she didn't move. Hans Overstreet stared first at Dan, then at the hard-looking woman at the bar, then back at Dan again. Dan said sharply, 'Jennie!'

She put her hands on the bar. Dan walked toward her slowly. When she was only a few feet away he asked, 'Where's the gun, Jennie?'

She turned her head and stared defiantly at him. He said harshly, 'The hard way or the easy. It makes no difference.'

She said, 'Holster on my left side.'

With his left hand, he reached out and raised the left side of her coat. He felt his hand close on the gun, but he couldn't draw it from the rear. He said, 'Turn real easy, Jennie. I don't want to hit you but I will if you force me to.'

She turned slowly toward him. He slipped the gun from its holster and jammed it into his hip pocket. He said softly, 'You're going to jail.'

'I'll tell them who you are.'

'I've already done that.'

She stared at him with shocked surprise and he said, 'You didn't think I would, did you?'

'It won't make any difference. Sam's not afraid of this town or of any other town. He'll still make his raid.'

'Maybe not. We'll see. In the meantime, you'll be in jail.'

91

She cursed him in a harshly savage voice. He took it silently. When she had finished, he nudged her toward the door with the muzzle of the gun. He followed her to the jail. Smead was still sitting at his desk. There was an angry scowl on his face.

Dan locked Jennie in a cell. He returned to the office, closing the door that separated it from the cells. He said, 'Don't let the fact that she's a woman fool you. She's as rough as any man.'

Smead nodded. He said, 'I'm going to have to tell the townspeople who you are. There's no other way.'

'I know.'

'They may insist that I lock you up. They may believe you brought the gang here.'

'I know that too.'

Smead got up, gesturing with his head toward the jail cells in the rear. 'Keep an eye on her. I'm going to get a few people and bring them here. I want you to tell them your story. Then we'll have to decide what we're going to do.'

The sheriff went out into the street. He paused there a moment, long enough to look up and down. Then he turned and headed uptown.

Dan began to pace nervously back and forth. He wondered what they'd do with him. Would they believe he'd had nothing to do with the gang's being here? Or would they think what Smead had said they might—that he was in with the gang and had brought them here? He shrugged fatalistically. Whatever they did, his own conscience was clear at least. He had told the sheriff the gang was in the area and he had given away their intention of robbing the Dobeville bank. Beyond that there was little he *could* do.

The sheriff was gone for what seemed a long time. In reality it was only about twenty minutes. When he returned, he had Ian Smitherman with him, and Hans Overstreet, and Charles Amherst, the minister, and Larry Widemeier, who owned the hotel. Behind this group were several others, including Ralph Morris, the town's attorney, and Doc Sinclair.

They all crowded into the office, nodding at Dan and speaking pleasantly to him. Dan realized the sheriff hadn't yet told them anything. Smead waited until the room had quieted and then he said, 'As you know, Dan's name is Youngerman. What you don't know is that Dan is a member of the notorious Youngerman family.'

There was a shocked silence that lasted several moments. Then everybody began talking at once. Dan felt like a bug mounted on a cork.

Smead raised his hands. 'You can talk later. Right now I want to tell you what Dan told me. Wilkes, the man that was killed by Frank Delaney the other night, was a member of the

Wilkes-Youngerman gang. He was here for the purpose of scouting the town for them.'

The silence within the little room was now complete. Nobody seemed to be breathing. Smead said, 'Dan backtracked him and found where the gang is camped. They are less than a dozen miles from town. They may raid the bank at any time.'

They were looking at Dan now, not at Smead. Ralph Morris asked, 'How many of them are there, Dan?'

'A dozen, maybe. I killed one when he jumped me out there near their camp. They sent a second man named Hawkins in yesterday and I pistol-whipped him and ran him out of town. This morning, Hugh Wilkes's sister Jennie is here to scout the town, and she's been asking questions about Frank. We put her in jail.'

'So there are probably ten men left in the gang at least.'

Dan nodded. 'That wouldn't miss it far.'

Morris stared steadily at him. Dan forced himself to meet the attorney's stare unflinchingly but it wasn't an easy thing to do. Morris asked, 'Why didn't you tell us this right after Wilkes was killed? We could have done several things if we'd known this a couple of days ago. We could have sent to Fort Dodge for troops. We could have made some plans, set up some kind of defense.'

Several of the others broke in. 'Yeah. Why

94

didn't you tell us this two days ago?'

Dan looked around at the hostile faces in the room. There was not a man who didn't wear an expression of suspicion. And he guessed he couldn't blame them much. He *had* kept Wilkes's identity a secret far too long. He had concealed the fact that the gang was waiting outside of town and by doing so had laid himself wide open to suspicion and criticism.

He said, 'You've known me for seven years. I've done my job. I've made friends in Dobeville. I've raised my family here.'

'Then why didn't you tell us? Why?'

'I guess I was afraid—that you'd think I was a member of the gang and had brought them here. And that's what you do think, isn't it?'

Doc Sinclair, a gaunt, aging man with sunken eyes, said, 'Can you blame us? You let two days go by without saying anything. Maybe you only spoke up now because you were afraid this Jennie Wilkes would get scared and give you away.'

Smead interrupted. 'Putting blame isn't going to get us anywhere. What we've got to decide is what we're going to do.'

There was a momentary silence. Then Ian Smitherman began to edge toward the door. 'I can tell you what I'm going to do. I'm going to draw my money out of the bank before the Youngerman gang gets it all.'

Others chimed in instantly, 'Yeah. Me too.'

95

Smead stood with his back to the door. 'Hold it! There's not going to be a run on the bank if I have to close it and keep it closed. Do you realize what will happen if everybody takes their money out?'

Morris said, 'The bank will go broke. But at least the townspeople will have the money instead of the Youngerman gang.'

'And for how long? When the gang comes in and finds the bank has been emptied, what do you think they'll do? They'll take hostages or burn the town, but they'll get that money from whoever has it. You can count on that.'

Dan nodded. 'He's right. They won't care what they have to do to force people to give up the money they have.'

'You'd like to see the money stay in the bank, wouldn't you?'

Dan looked pleadingly at Smead. Smead said, 'Nothing's going to be gained by blaming Dan. Maybe he was late in telling us. But he told us, and you've got to admit he could have kept still until it was too late. I've known Dan for seven years and I believe in him.'

There was no agreement from the other men in the room. They stared at Dan with open hostility. They were scared and they needed somebody to blame, and Dan was it.

CHAPTER TWELVE

Smead looked around at the ring of hostile faces for a long time. At last he said, 'We're only talking about ten men, even if they are outlaws. We can defend the town. We can stop the Youngerman gang in its tracks.'

'The same way Lawrence stopped Quantrill, I suppose.'

'Lawrence didn't know Quantrill was coming, and besides, Quantrill had over a hundred men.'

'Lawrence was a hell of a lot bigger than Dobeville, too.'

Smead looked at the faces of the men disgustedly. 'What do you want to do, then?'

Doc Sinclair said, 'How do we know, Luke? You're the one who's supposed to keep the peace. First of all, I think you ought to lock Dan up. At least until we've made up our minds.'

Smead stared at Doc angrily. 'You can go to hell. I need Dan. I sure as hell am not going to get much help from anyone else, if the rest of the men in town are like you.'

Sinclair said, 'Let's get Ned Winslow and Harry Cooper down here and talk to them. Let's find out how much money is in the bank.'

'What good is that going to do?'

'Maybe we can afford to lose the money easier than we can afford to lose the whole town and some lives to boot.'

Smead stared at him pityingly. 'That's a chicken-livered statement if I ever heard one. Are you suggesting that we just let Sam Youngerman have what he wants?'

'Maybe it's better than putting up a fight. The town is worth more than what money is in the bank.'

Smead said, 'All right, go get Cooper and Winslow. Let's see what they've got to say.'

Doc Sinclair didn't move. He said, 'Send Dan after them.'

For a moment, Smead seemed about to refuse. Then he turned his head and looked at Dan. 'Get them, will you, Dan?'

Dan went out into the bright sunlight. He closed the door behind him. He was angry now. He didn't know what he'd expected from the town, but he had thought some of the people would believe in him.

He walked quickly across the street to the bank. He went inside. There were no customers in the lobby. Ned Winslow was in the teller's cage. Dan didn't see Harry Cooper, but he supposed he was somewhere in the back. Dan said, 'The sheriff wants you and Harry down at the office, Ned. Can you lock up for a few minutes and come? It's important.'

Ned looked at him uncertainly for a moment. Then he said, 'I'll ask Mr. Cooper.' He disappeared and Dan heard voices in the rear of the bank. A few moments later, Harry

Cooper and Ned came through the brass-grille gate. Harry Cooper stared at Dan. 'What's this all about?'

'The sheriff will tell you. He just asked me to bring you down.'

Cooper shrugged. He was a thickset, graying man in his late fifties, dressed conservatively in a dark blue suit. He put on his hat and followed Dan and Ned Winslow out the door. Turning, he locked it and walked along the street beside Dan. Winslow walked behind the two because the walk was too narrow for three abreast.

Cooper asked, 'This isn't going to take long, is it, Dan?'

'I don't think so.'

They crossed the street to the sheriff's office. Dan opened the door and Cooper went in, followed by Winslow and then by Dan. Dan pulled the door shut behind him. Cooper looked at Smead. 'Dan says you want to see us.'

Smead nodded. 'I'll fill you in a little. Dan is a brother of the Youngermans who belong to that outlaw gang. He tells us that the gang is within a dozen miles of town and that they're here to raid your bank.'

Cooper lost color. He looked at the other men in the room as if wondering what they were doing here. Smead went on, 'I'm sorry to have to hit you with it so suddenly, Mr. Cooper, but we don't have much time.'

Cooper glanced at Dan, then back at Smead. 'Why has the gang picked Dobeville to raid?'

Smead looked questioningly at Dan. Dan said, 'It's a personal thing between Sam and me.'

Cooper said firmly, 'I think we have a right to know.'

Dan nodded reluctantly. 'I guess you do. It's Sarah. She was promised to Sam originally, but when I came home from the war . . . well, we fell in love. We told Sam and right afterward we got married. He didn't take it very well. He swore he'd have revenge against me before he was through. I guess this is his revenge. He can't kill me because we're brothers. But if he raids Dobeville, he figures the town will accuse me of being part of his gang, maybe even of bringing him here. He figures I'll either be lynched or sent to prison.'

Cooper nodded. 'All right. I understand. I presume you want to station armed men within the bank. You have my consent.'

Smead shook his head. 'That isn't exactly it, Harry.' He looked challengingly at Doc Sinclair. 'Suppose you explain it to him, Doc. I think you understand it a little better than I do.'

Doc glanced at Cooper almost guiltily. 'How much cash money have you got in the bank?'

Cooper frowned. He said, 'That's none of your business, Dr. Sinclair.'

Smead let Doc flounder on. Doc said, 'I know you don't like to let a thing like that out, and maybe it isn't any of our business. But we have to know. It's important. We can't make an intelligent decision unless we do know.'

'Are you suggesting that we let the Wilkes-Youngerman gang have what's in the bank?'

Doc's face was defiant. 'Isn't that better than letting them burn the town? I've heard about that Quantrill raid, Mr. Cooper, even if you haven't. I don't want to see it happen here.'

'That was different. Quantrill had over a hundred men.'

'And Lawrence was a bigger town.'

Smead broke in. 'We're not getting anyplace with this. Tell him how much money is in the bank safe, Mr. Cooper and let's get on with it.'

'I don't know exactly. Forty or fifty thousand dollars, I suppose.'

Doc Sinclair whistled. 'Whew! I didn't know it would be that much.'

Harry Cooper looked around. 'Last year was a good crop year. People have been paying off their loans.'

Smead stared at Doc Sinclair. 'Suppose we do let the Youngermans have the money in the bank? Who's going to take the loss?'

'All of us, I suppose. Everybody in Dobeville.'

'On what ratio? Equal shares? Or do you suggest we prorate it?'

'Prorate it, I suppose.'

'On what basis, for Christ's sake? And how long do you think we'll have to argue about it before everybody agrees? The Youngerman gang will have the money and have it spent before we agree on how to prorate the loss.'

There was silence for a moment. The occupants of the room stared at each other. From outside in the street a strange noise came, almost immediately recognizable as dozens of voices speaking or shouting at once. Dan looked toward the window. Downstreet, from the direction of the Free State Saloon, he could see a group of men approaching the jail. He got up, went to the door and opened it, then stepped out onto the walk.

The sound was plainer now, and loud, and individual voices were recognizable even if their words were not. Dan's stomach suddenly felt empty because when the members of the crowd saw him the tone of their voices changed.

Smead came out and stood beside him. The others also crowded out. John Temple, leading the crowd, yelled, 'You know who you got for a deputy, Luke?'

Smead nodded. 'I know. I've known him for seven years and so have you.'

'Do you know he's a brother to Sam Youngerman?'

Smead nodded.

'Well, for Christ's sake, what are you going

to do about it?'

'What do you think I ought to do?'

'Throw him in jail, that's what! There's probably a price on his head just like there is on the rest of the Youngermans.'

'Why should there be? He's not a member of the gang.'

'How do you know he's not?'

'Because of what he's been telling us. The Youngerman gang is less than a dozen miles from town right now. They're going to raid the bank.'

For several moments there was silence in the street. Then a man yelled, 'Then he probably brought them here!'

Dan looked toward the sound of the voice, but he couldn't decide which of them had yelled that out. It didn't matter anyway, because it was apparent that several of the men agreed.

Smead yelled, 'Go home! Get off the street! I may call on you later when we've decided what we're going to do!'

John Temple yelled, 'You're not going to let Dan know what you decide, are you? How do you know he won't tell the gang?'

Smead didn't answer. He just shook his head disgustedly.

Temple said defiantly, 'He was with Quantrill during the war, wasn't he? Maybe the rest of you don't know what happened there.'

103

Smead said sourly, 'That happened during the war and the war's been over for seven years.'

Dan said, 'I'll leave. I don't mind.'

Temple was scowling savagely at Dan. 'Sure you'll leave. Sure. And while we're down here trying to decide what to do, you'll be sending word out to the Youngerman gang.'

The crowd howled agreement. Smead yelled, 'Oh for God's sake, shut up!' He turned his head and looked at Dan. 'Go on home for a while, Dan. There's no reason why you have to listen to this kind of abuse.'

He pushed through the angry crowd and untied his horse. He mounted and reined the animal roughly around, not caring that the horse almost knocked John Temple off his feet. Temple glared up at him but he did not accept the challenge in Dan's eyes.

Dan trotted the horse up Main, which was virtually deserted except for the crowd in front of the jail.

There was a little knot of women standing in front of Smitherman's. They stared at him but he couldn't tell whether they knew who he really was or not.

It was a big temptation to just leave town. He felt like hitching up the buckboard and throwing a couple of suitcases in the back and leaving. Right now. Today.

He turned his head and scowled back at the crowd collected in front of the jail. He felt like leaving, but he knew that he could not. Leaving would be an admission of guilt. They'd probably demand that Smead swear out a warrant for his arrest. He'd be a fugitive.

The townsmen were scared and they had good reason to be scared. Just the thought of the Wilkes-Youngerman gang was enough to scare anyone. The gang was vicious and had left other towns burning in the past. It was one of Sam's favorite tricks. Leave people fighting to save their homes and their businesses and they couldn't get up a posse and chase him until it was too late.

He rode up the alley and put the horse into the stable. He didn't want to go in the house. He didn't want to tell Sarah how the townspeople had reacted to knowing who he was. Nor did he want to frighten the children. He realized that, as upset as he was, he couldn't help but communicate what he was feeling to them, even if they didn't understand.

Irritably he paced back and forth, wondering how long it was going to take the townspeople to decide what they were going to do. He didn't see how they could do anything but fight. He couldn't believe that those like Doc who wanted to give in to the gang would prevail.

This was a golden opportunity for the people of Dobeville.

Sam Youngerman usually struck unexpectedly, but the people of Dobeville were forewarned. If they had the courage to fight, they could destroy the Youngerman gang, once and for all. They could earn the respect and gratitude of the whole frontier.

He hoped he could make them see that, after they had calmed down, after their first panic had disappeared. But he didn't really believe he could.

CHAPTER THIRTEEN

Apparently Sarah had heard him in the stable. The back screen door slammed and she called, 'Dan? Is that you?'

He stepped out into the yard. 'Uh huh.'

Her expression was concerned. 'Why are you home? What's happening? I thought I heard a lot of yelling from the direction of town a while ago.'

'You did.' He felt his thoughts turning sour as he remembered how ready they had been to condemn. Maybe they were scared but that didn't excuse some of the things they had said to him.

Sarah seemed to understand the sourness of his thoughts. 'Is there anything I can do to help?'

He shook his head. 'There's a crowd down at the jail and some of the leading citizens are talking it out with Smead. Some of them want

106

to let Sam have what's in the bank without even putting up a fight.'

She stared at him unbelievingly. 'If they do that, it will be impossible for us to stay. They'll blame you for the rest of your life. They'll blame me and they'll even blame the kids.'

'I know it.'

'Sam's only a man. He's not invincible.'

'They've heard stories about the other towns he's raided. They know how he operates. They don't want him to burn Dobeville.'

'He can't if they put up a fight.'

Dan shook his head. 'Yes, he can. And he will too. The minute someone opens up on him he'll withdraw and set fires at the edge of town. Then while the townspeople are fighting fires, he'll finish at the bank.'

'Did they give you a bad time?'

He grinned ruefully.

'Why did you come home?'

'Luke sent me. He said I shouldn't have to listen to any more of their abuse.'

'At least he's standing back of you.'

Dan nodded. Luke was standing back of him right now but that didn't mean he would continue to do so indefinitely. The pressure might become too great.

Frowning, he wondered when Sam would make the raid. Tomorrow morning, he supposed. When Jennie didn't come back this afternoon, he'd know she was either dead or in jail. Knowing that, he would figure he couldn't

107

afford to wait. Sam didn't want to tangle with a troop of cavalry from Fort Dodge.

Sarah said, 'I've got some coffee on the stove.'

He walked to the back door with her and followed her inside. There was an increasingly determined look in her eyes as she filled a cup for him, and an increasingly firm set to her mouth and chin. Her face was slightly flushed. She said, 'I think we ought to leave. Why should we stay here if they don't think any more of us than to accuse you of the things they have?'

Dan sipped his coffee. He glanced up and saw that her eyes were sparkling with anger at the town. He said, 'We can't leave them now. It's because of us that they're in trouble. Regardless of what they've said, we still live here. We can't let them down.'

'I don't see why not!'

He went on, 'If we leave, this thing will follow us for the rest of our lives. But if we stay, and if the town defeats Sam, we'll be all through running, and hiding, and living in fear.'

'But you said . . .'

'I know. The townspeople are scared and want to quit. But Luke will talk them out of it.'

She looked at him doubtfully. 'I hope so. When do you think Sam will come?'

'Tomorrow. In the morning, probably.' He finished the coffee and got up. He began to pace nervously back and forth. He heard footsteps upstairs, and heard the children's voices. A few moments later the two children came downstairs. They came to him and he gathered them up in his arms.

If there had been any doubts in him as to the wisdom of staying, the children's arms around his neck would have driven them away. He couldn't subject them to a nomadic life of moving from place to place while the stigma of his name followed them.

He put the children down and glanced at his wife. 'Well, they ought to have their minds made up by now. I suppose I'd better go back down to the office and find out what their decision was.'

'What if they still refuse to fight?'

His mouth firmed out. 'Then I guess I'll have to go out to Sam's camp myself. I'll . . .'

'No, Dan. He's your brother.'

He looked at her steadily. 'And you're my wife. And these are my two kids.'

Danny piped up, 'Daddy, who's Sam?'

Dan said, 'Never mind.' He kissed Sarah lightly on the mouth. 'I'll come and tell you as soon as I know anything.'

She nodded and he went out the back door. He went to the stable and led his horse out into the alley behind the house. He mounted and rode back toward Main.

There was a strange excitement in the town of Dobeville now. Women were clustered in small groups on porches, sidewalks, and lawns. The voices of children were strangely still. Even the dogs seemed to have forgotten how to bark.

Main Street was virtually empty along most of its length. But down at the jail, the crowd remained, forming a half circle in front. Apparently the discussion was still going on inside. Evidently the prominent citizens of the town had not yet decided what should be done.

When the crowd saw Dan, some men began to yell. Grant Flood, the blacksmith, bawled, 'There's the traitor now! Let's fix him so's he can't help his murderin' brothers rob the bank!'

Dan rode deliberately toward Flood. The blacksmith was one man in town with whom he had never gotten along. He didn't like Flood any better than Flood liked him.

The crowd gave before him, except for Flood. Dan kept a tight rein, forcing his horse directly at the blacksmith. The horse's shoulder nudged him and pushed him back. Dan stared steadily at Flood, daring him to retaliate.

Suddenly Flood seized his leg. The man weighed more than two hundred pounds and he yanked Dan from the saddle as if he had been a child. Dan felt himself falling and an instant later felt the wind driven from his lungs as he landed on his back in the dust.

He rolled instinctively, hugging his belly with his arms. Flood's kick struck his right

110

forearm and for a moment Dan thought he had broken it.

But he was ready for the next kick when it came. He seized Flood's heavy boot and hugged it to his belly, at the same time rolling violently away.

Flood was neatly dumped into the dust. Dan was still gasping for the breath knocked out of him by the fall, but he made it to his hands and knees and peered sideways at Flood, hoping the blacksmith would stay down long enough for him to fill his lungs.

Gasping, he circled warily. The crowd moved back and formed an arena for the two in the dusty street. They were mostly silent, perhaps startled that Flood would attack a representative of the law, but Dan guessed their surprise wouldn't last very long. He had to take care of Flood quickly and ruthlessly, or others might join with him. Once they had manhandled him successfully, their respect for him would be forever gone.

Flood rushed, unhurt, and apparently as anxious as Dan to see an end to this. Dan waited, standing fast, until Flood had almost reached him. Then, leaping to one side, he brought his right fist and forearm down like a sledge against the back of the blacksmith's thick neck as Flood went past.

His whole arm turned numb, but he was gratified to see Flood stumble and fall, face downward, in the dust. Dan gave him no time to recover or regain his feet. Drawing his gun, he stepped to the blacksmith's side, and as he came groggily to his feet, rammed the gun savagely into Flood's side. 'Keep your hands down and go on in the jail! You're under arrest!'

Flood turned his head and glared. There was dust all over his face and on his clothes. He wasn't hurt and he wasn't beaten, but Dan had, at least, regained the upper hand.

For an instant, rebellion flared in the blacksmith's eyes. Dan jabbed the gun barrel deeper into his ribs, forcing a grunt of pain from Flood. He said, 'Don't! You're in custody. I don't want to pull this trigger but I will if you force me to.'

He could see the fight drain out of Flood, along with the color that drained out of his face. He must have convinced the man that he'd do exactly what he had threatened, because Flood marched meekly toward the door of the jail.

It stood open. Smead was framed in it. Smead was scowling but his eyes gave Dan such an abundance of approval that Dan couldn't help grinning at him. Prodding Flood with the muzzle of his gun, Dan marched him across the office and through the door leading to the cells. He gestured toward a barred door standing open on the opposite side of the corridor from the cell occupied by Jennie Wilkes. 'In there.'

Flood went in. Dan holstered his gun, slammed the door, locked it, and pocketed the key. He returned to the office, brushing the dust from his clothes. He went outside and tied his horse to the rail. His expression dared those in the street to say anything.

He came back into the office and closed the door. His eyes questioned the sheriff, but Smead glanced around at the men inside the office instead of answering. Smead said, 'There's not much time to make up your minds. Sam Youngerman will likely hit the bank tonight or early tomorrow morning. If you think he won't burn the town just because you let him have the bank, then you're out of your minds. He's mean and full of hate. One of his cousins has been killed here and we have another locked in jail. He'll burn Dobeville out of pure cussedness, no matter what we do.'

'What do *you* think we ought to do?'

'There aren't but two things we *can* do. One is to have Dan lead us out to Sam Youngerman's camp and attack him there. The other is to lay an ambush in town and wait for him.'

'What about troops from Fort Dodge?'

'I'll send for them but I don't think they can get here in time.'

Doc Sinclair said, 'I still think . . .'

Harry Cooper said harshly, 'Shut up, Doc! We don't give a damn what you think.' He looked at Smead. 'Why don't you go ahead and

113

send for troops? We can talk about this afterward.'

Smead glanced at Dan. 'Go down to the telegraph office and get the telegram off, will you, Dan? Just say we've seen the Youngerman gang near Dobeville and figure they're going to raid the bank. Ask for a troop of cavalry as soon as possible.'

Dan nodded. He went out, untied his horse, mounted, and rode through the crowd, which opened a path for him silently. His treatment of Flood had restored his authority, if only temporarily. They grumbled, but nobody said anything that he could understand.

He rode down the middle of Main to the depot at its lower end. He dismounted at the platform and tied his horse to an iron ring placed there for that purpose. He climbed the steps and went into the station.

The telegraph key was silent but that wasn't unusual. Gus Shipley glanced up at him from the pile of papers on his desk. Dan said, 'The sheriff wants to send a telegram to the commandant at Fort Dodge. Get it off right away.'

'Write it out.'

Dan picked up a pad of telegram blanks and scrawled the message with a pencil stub. Gus read it briefly, then went to his key. It clicked rapidly for several moments, then stopped. It clicked again for several moments, then stopped again. Gus looked up, frowning

114

perplexedly. He said, 'I can't send any telegrams. The wires are down somewhere. The damn thing's dead.'

Dan nodded. He was not surprised. Sam had cut the wires to keep a call for help from going to Fort Dodge. Sam was ready to attack.

CHAPTER FOURTEEN

Dan left the railroad station. Behind him, Gus Shipley looked scared. Dan untied his horse, mounted, and headed back uptown. He couldn't help glancing eastward in the direction from which Sam and the gang would come. Nor could he help wondering how the town would take the news that the telegraph wires were down, that no help was coming from Fort Dodge.

The crowd in front of the jail had grown. Dan supposed Smead had told them about the telegram and he knew the sheriff wouldn't want him to tell them the wires had been cut. Not yet. Gus Shipley would probably leak the news before long but maybe by the time he did, Smead would have the townspeople organized.

Someone yelled, 'How long will it take the soldiers, Dan?'

He glanced toward the voice and shrugged. Another man, somewhere in the crowd yelled,

'How the hell do we even know he sent the telegram?'

Still a third voice yelled, 'Go ask Gus!'

Dan didn't wait to see if anybody headed for the depot. He went into the sheriff's office. Smead glanced at him and Dan said, 'The wires are down. They probably were cut.'

Doc Sinclair let out a groan of despair.

Smead said, 'I don't know what difference it makes. We couldn't have gotten soldiers here soon enough anyway. And maybe it's time we faced the truth. We're on our own. It's going to be up to us to stop the Youngerman gang. Have any of you ever thought how much wiping out the gang will do for Dobeville? This will be the most famous town in the whole United States.'

'Or it'll be a pile of ashes.'

Dan felt his face heating up. He looked straight at Doc. 'You've been doing a lot of spouting off. Why don't you shut up long enough for somebody else to say something?'

Doc turned his furious gaze on Dan, who met it unflinchingly. Harry Cooper said, 'Dan's right. Let's hear what the others have to say. I'll go on record as wanting to fight off the gang. They're mean enough to burn the town whether we put up a fight or not. But if we fight, maybe we can drive them off.'

Smead looked around at the others. 'All right. Speak up. What do the rest of you want to do?'

116

Before they could answer, the door opened. Amanda Foster, a spinster who ran a dress shop up the street from the hotel, was there. She looked at the sheriff, then at Cooper and Winslow. 'Isn't the bank going to open up? I need some change. Mrs. Satterlee is in my shop waiting.'

Cooper said, 'Go on down and open up, Ned. I'll be there as soon as I can get away.'

Winslow went to the door. 'Come on, Miss Foster. I'll open the bank for you.'

As the door was closing, Dan heard her shrill voice, 'What's going on, for heaven's sake? This is the first time I can remember that the bank hasn't opened up on time, and what's that crowd doing in the street?'

Sinclair said, 'I've had my say. I'm leaving.' He went to the door and hurried out. He turned in the direction in which Winslow and Amanda Foster had disappeared. Smitherman said, 'I guess I've got to agree with Doc. I sure as hell don't want my store burned. I'd rather lose what money I've got in the bank.' He was staring at the door. 'No use me staying here. I've said what I had to say.' He went out, and turned in the direction Doc had gone.

Ralph Morris said, 'I think I have to agree with Doc and with Smitherman. Excuse me, gentlemen.'

Morris was a tall, thin, middle-aged man, who somehow managed to seem courtly under any circumstances. He favored gray in his

117

dress, and had the slightest of soft Missouri accents. Morris went out and turned toward the bank.

Dan said, 'You can see what they're up to, can't you? Ned just left to open the bank for Amanda Foster. Those three are headed up there to get their money out before you close the bank.'

Smead's face was grim. 'Come on, Harry. You too, Dan. Let's get over there before we have a damned riot on our hands.'

He went out of the office, hurrying. Harry Cooper followed and Dan waited until the remaining townsmen went out. Then he locked the office door. They still had Jennie Wilkes and Flood in jail.

Smead and Cooper were halfway to the bank, running. The crowd that had been in front of the jail had almost reached the bank ahead of them. Amanda Foster, Ned Winslow, Doc Sinclair, Smitherman, and Morris had disappeared.

Dan broke into a run. The crowd closed ranks in front of the bank, jamming the door, and blocking the sheriff and Cooper from entering. Dan saw the two round the corner, obviously heading for the alley door.

He cut through a vacant lot diagonally, and met them behind the bank. Cooper was unlocking the back door of the bank. Smead said, 'Stay here, Dan. Don't let anyone come in.'

Dan pulled the door closed and put his back to it. The sheriff and Cooper sure had their work cut out for them, getting that scared bunch of people out of the bank.

From inside of the bank, he suddenly heard a low roar, the sound of many shouts mingling. He smiled grimly to himself. He had hoped the town would close ranks and fight off the Youngermans when they knew their peril. Instead they were fighting each other, clawing their way toward the teller's cage, each trying to get his own money out of the bank before the Youngerman gang arrived. No one wanted to fight.

Suddenly, muffled, from inside the bank, Dan heard a shot. He heard a voice shouting, also muffled by the walls of the bank. He opened the back door slightly and listened.

Smead was yelling furiously at them, and cursing, which was something Dan had never heard him do. Trying to get them out of the bank, Dan thought. Trying, but not having much success.

He backed into the door, closing it behind him. There was a bolt on the inside. He bolted the door and moved toward the front of the bank. Smead and Cooper needed help. He understood why Smead had left him to guard the door. The sheriff hadn't wanted anybody to be able to accuse him of wanting to keep the money in the bank so that it would be there when the Youngerman gang arrived. Now it didn't matter. If the sheriff and Cooper didn't get that mob out of the bank soon, there wasn't going to be any bank.

Again, Dan heard a shot, this time deafening. He saw a cloud of blue powder smoke billow toward the high ceiling above the teller's cage, saw plaster sift down from the place the bullet had entered it.

He broke into a run, drawing his gun as he did. Smead stood on the left side of the lobby, just beyond the brass-grille gate. Cooper was in the teller's cage with Ned Winslow, who looked white and scared. Ian Smitherman was in front of the cage, yelling at Cooper and Winslow.

Dan came up behind Smead. 'What do you want me to do?'

'Get over there in the teller's cage. Get the money from Ned and take it back and put it in the safe. Maybe when they realize they can't get to the money, they'll give up and leave.'

Dan hurried to the teller's cage. He said, 'The sheriff told me to get the money from you and lock it in the safe.'

Winslow hastily scooped it out of the drawer and dumped it into a canvas sack. He threw the sack at Dan, who retreated with it toward the safe. A dozen men had seized the brass grille and were rocking it back and forth. In an instant it was going to break and Dan knew he'd be overwhelmed.

He reached the safe and threw the sack

inside, beside half a dozen other sacks. He could see a shelf neatly stacked with packages of greenbacks, bound together with paper strips.

The grillwork gave with a crash. Dan slammed the safe door, locked the handle, then twirled the dial. He turned as the first of the crowd reached him. Looking over their heads, he saw that Smead was surrounded, as were Cooper and Ned Winslow.

Dan stood with his back to the safe. 'Too late,' he shouted. 'You'd better start thinking about fighting off that gang instead of worrying about getting your money out of the bank. It's in the safe and it'll stay there until the Youngermans blow the door.'

They jostled against him and a couple of them yanked at the handle angrily. But up front, Smead and Cooper were at last getting them out of the bank. The crowd continued to thin until at last they were all gone.

Cooper stared at the wrecked grillwork, then at Smead, then at Dan. He said, 'I don't know how many of the others are going to fight, but you can count on Ned and me. Just give us guns and tell us what to do.'

Smead nodded. 'Nothing's likely to happen until evening. Come down to the jail an hour before dark.'

He went out, with Dan following him. The crowd had not dispersed. They still filled the street. They still were in an ugly mood. They glared at Dan and at Smead, blaming the sheriff not only because he was supporting his deputy, but also because they had to blame somebody. They had formed little groups to discuss the situation among themselves.

Dan and Smead walked to the jail. Dan unlocked the door and they went inside. Dan said ruefully, 'It's too bad they wouldn't turn some of that anger on the Youngermans.'

Smead snorted. 'Well, we've got two men, at least,' he said.

'Four isn't going to be enough.'

'I know it. But give 'em a little time to get over being scared.' He went to the rear of the office and opened the door leading to the cells. Immediately Grant Flood's voice said, 'Lemme out of here, sheriff. You got no right to hold me in jail.'

'Shut up, Flood. You know better than that. I'll hold you as long as I want.'

'What's the charge, sheriff? You can't hold me without a charge. I know my rights.'

'All right then. Assaulting an officer. Interfering with an officer in the performance of his duty. Inciting to riot. Disturbing the peace. How's that for a starter?'

'You can't make any one of them charges stick. Dan started it.'

'I don't have to make them stick to hold you in jail. Now shut up unless you want something.'

'You can't make me shut up.'

Smead stared at him silently. Flood subsided into a resentful mumbling. The sheriff glanced at Jennie Wilkes. 'Anything I can get for you, ma'am?'

She looked up at him, her eyes smoldering. She did not reply. Smead closed the door and crossed to his desk. The oak swivel chair creaked as he sat down.

A horse pounded to a halt outside. Dan glanced up as Frank Delaney burst through the office door. He said disgustedly, 'I thought you'd be miles away from here by now.'

Delaney asked, 'On what? I ain't got but thirty cents. A man can't eat long on thirty cents. I want part of that reward. I want enough so I can eat.'

'Or so you can keep yourself supplied with whisky.' Dan was thoroughly disgusted. He'd gone to a lot of trouble getting Delaney to leave town. He looked at the sheriff. Smead fished a leather pocketbook out and opened it. He took out two twenty-dollar gold pieces. 'I've got forty dollars, Frank. You're welcome to it, but it's all I can give you. At least until the reward comes through officially.'

'How far will forty dollars go?' Delaney was sullen, and it was obvious that he was still sick from the drink he'd been on the night before.

'Maybe far enough to keep you from getting your head blown off.'

Dan said, 'Far enough if you don't drink it up.'

123

'It ain't enough. By God, it ain't enough.'

Smead said, 'Get out of here, Frank. If you want to stay in town and get killed, I guess that's your business. But get out of here and stop bothering me. I've got work to do.'

'Well, gimme the forty dollars, then.'

Silently, Smead handed him the two coins. Delaney went out, scowling. He slammed the door savagely.

Dan said, 'He won't leave town. He'll go down to the Free State and get himself drunk all over again.'

The sheriff shrugged. He grinned ruefully at Dan. 'Maybe I just want to feel I've done what I could.'

Dan stared through the window at the crowds milling in the street. He said sourly, 'There are enough men out there to slaughter the Youngerman gang. But I'll bet that when the chips are down, we don't get six.'

CHAPTER FIFTEEN

For several minutes Smead and Dan stood side by side staring out the window into the street. At last Smead said, 'Go on up to the bank. Pick out four or five of the best vantage points. Try to find some that will cover every possible escape route the gang might take getting away from the bank. If they're going to withdraw when we open fire on them and try setting fire to the town, I want to be able to cut them to pieces when they do.'

Dan nodded. Smead said, 'While you're doing that, I'm going out there and pick the likeliest men I can find. I'm going to put it straight to them, that I'm forming a posse and they either join it or face prosecution.'

'Might work. It's worth a try.'

Before leaving, Dan walked to the door opening into the rear and called, 'Anything you two need?'

Jennie said, 'You might bring me a screen so this big ape won't be looking at me all the time.'

Dan grinned. 'I'll bring it when I come back. It'll be fifteen or twenty minutes. Is that all right?'

She grumbled something but he couldn't tell what it had been. He followed the sheriff into the street, locking the door behind him. Smead crossed diagonally, heading for the nearest group of men. Dan headed for the bank.

The balcony over its entrance was only for looks, but the windows behind it formed excellent vantage points. They covered two directions perfectly. The only trouble was, the gang's fire would be concentrated on those windows, and if it was heavy enough, whoever was stationed there would be forced to stay down out of sight.

Diagonally across from the bank was a two-story office building jammed up against the north wall of Smitherman's furniture store. There was a narrow passage between the two buildings that was not more than a foot wide. A man could stand in that passageway and command Fourth Street to the east, and Main Street toward the lower end of town. There were windows along both Fourth Street and Main on the second story of the building.

Directly across from the bank was a one-story, false-fronted building that housed the office of the Booth County Abstract Company. Men could be stationed on the roof and be unseen behind the building's high false front. On the fourth corner of the intersection, diagonally across from the Abstract Company's office was the Booth Hotel, a brick, two-story building now vacant. It could also be used to conceal riflemen and its brick walls would provide more protection than would the frame walls of the other buildings.

In these four buildings, then, the defenders would have to be stationed. If enough could be recruited, Dan figured they should also station men both in the rear second-story windows above the bank and also in the rear second-story windows of the office building diagonally across the street so that if the retreating gang tried to cut down either alley, they would be exposed to fire from those vantage points.

Frowning, Dan stared at the intersection and at the buildings facing it. There ought to be at least two men in the bank, two in the office building, two in the abandoned Booth Hotel, and two on the roof of the abstract company. That would be eight. In addition, there should be one in the passageway between Smitherman's and the office building, and two in its rear windows, two more in the rear upstairs windows above the bank. Thirteen men in all.

The mob that had earlier jammed the bank and wrecked the grillwork, had withdrawn to the front of the hotel. A few were in the vacant lot between the hotel and the bank. There was some talking among them, but mostly they just stared at Dan as if he was personally to blame for what was happening. For a moment he looked back at them.

He knew each one. Most of them he liked. But theirs were not the faces that he knew. Without exception they were angry, hostile, and suspicious.

Cooper had locked the doors of the bank. He had put the 'closed' sign in the door. He had drawn the green blinds on the windows so that no one could see in.

Dan went into the hotel. Larry Widemeier was standing at one of the big front windows staring at the crowd. Dan said, 'We've got a woman prisoner in the jail and we need a screen to give her privacy. Can I borrow one of these?' He gestured with his head toward one of the folding screens that stood between the desk and the lobby.

Widemeier nodded. Dan crossed the lobby, folded one of the screens, and carried it outside. He crossed the street with it and went into the jail.

Smead glanced up. 'Well?'

'Wait until I give this to Jennie. She was complaining that there wasn't any privacy.'

He took the screen back into the corridor between the cells and put it up so that it separated Jennie's cell from that of Flood. Flood stared at him sulkily. Jennie did not look up.

He returned to the office and closed the door. He told Smead how he had figured out the bank's defense. He said, 'We need a hell of a good shot between Smitherman's and that office building on the corner.'

Smead said, 'All right. That's your spot. Unless you think you can't gun down your own kinfolk.'

Dan's chest felt empty. His stomach felt as if it had a big rock in it. He looked at the sheriff, steadily holding the sheriff's glance. 'I think I can but I'm not sure. Put yourself in my shoes, Luke. How can I know? I don't want you to put me in a spot that's as crucial as that one is. I think you're the one that ought to be in that passageway. I can be up on a roof someplace.'

Smead's expression said he wanted to believe in Dan. It also said he was having trouble doing it. Dan said, 'If it's going to help, just put me in jail until it's all over with.'

Smead scowled and shook his head.

Dan remembered the sheriff had gone out to recruit a posse. He asked, 'How many men did you get?'

For a moment, Smead did not reply and Dan knew what the answer would be even before he spoke. Smead said, 'None.'

'Did you tell them they'd face prosecution if they refused?'

'Sure I told them. But they told me to go to hell. They're half-scared to death. It's like they knew Quantrill was coming here instead of the Youngermans.'

'Well, we've got Cooper and Ned Winslow and you and me. That's four, at least.'

'Four won't be enough. Four will just infuriate that gang. Four will only hurt them enough to make them burn the town. If we can't get more than four, I think we'd better just let them have the money in the bank.'

Dan looked questioningly at him. 'That doesn't sound like you.'

'You didn't talk to that bunch of bastards out there in the street.'

Suddenly Dan heard a shout in the street. For an instant, there was a chunk of ice in his chest. Had the gang come early? Was that what the shouting meant?

He rushed outside. A man was running up the middle of the street from the direction of the depot. He was Ev Mason, who had a small grocery store over on Elm, half a block above the depot. He yelled hoarsely, 'The telegraph wires have been cut! They've cut the telegraph wires so's we can't get help from Dodge!'

Behind Dan, Smead said, 'Oh hell! The fat's in the fire now!'

Mason halted in front of the jail. He yelled, 'Did you know the telegraph wires were down, sheriff, or didn't your deputy tell you that?'

Smead said, 'He told me but I didn't tell the rest of you because I knew you'd panic if I did.'

Men were coming now from everywhere, converging on the jail. They were scared men but they were angry too. One yelled, 'Smead, it's time you got rid of him!'

Smead waited a moment, until the cries of agreement died away. Then he shouted, 'Get one thing through your heads. I'm not getting rid of Dan, because I need him. Now if you'll all calm down, I'll send him along with three or four of you to find the break in the telegraph line and splice it so we can get a message through. Not that it will do us any good. Troops can't get here until tomorrow afternoon and that will likely be too late.'

They stared at the sheriff and at Dan sullenly. Smead yelled, 'Tinker, Maxwell, and Olivares. Get horses and be ready to go. Dan will stop by the telegraph office for wire and some tools. Meet him there in fifteen minutes.'

The men broke away from the crowd and hurried toward their homes.

130

Smead said, 'Go ahead, Dan. Tell Gus Shipley to get that telegram off the minute you get the wire fixed.'

Dan nodded. He didn't really want to leave but he knew Smead wanted him to go. He wanted the town to simmer down and he knew they'd be less afraid if they knew a message had reached the fort.

Dan felt like part of the community for the first time today. Smead trusted him or he wouldn't send him to splice the break in the telegraph line.

He mounted his horse and rode down the street to the depot. Gus Shipley was standing on the platform. Dan said, 'I want wire and splicing tools and some climbers. We're going out and try to find the break. Smead says to get that message off to the commandant at Fort Dodge just as soon as the line is fixed.'

Shipley went inside. Dan dismounted and tied his horse. He followed the telegrapher into the depot.

Shipley found the wire and tools he had asked for and helped him carry them outside. Juan Olivares was already waiting and by the time Dan had stowed the tools in his saddlebags and hung the wire over the saddle horn, the others had arrived.

He mounted and led east out of town, following the telegraph line which itself followed the railroad tracks. Aware that time was short, he lifted his horse to an easy,

131

rocking lope.

Silently, the others followed him. He supposed they distrusted him too, but that couldn't be helped, and anyway he was getting to a point where he didn't care whether they trusted him or not. He had done all he could, and maybe they wouldn't fully trust him until he stood in a window looking down into the street and helped them cut the gang to bits.

A mile dropped behind, a second, and a third. Dan began to wonder how far they would have to go before they found the break. Sam had probably cut it near his camp and that was ten miles from town. Dan didn't really want to take that much time finding and fixing it because it was possible that Sam and the others would attack the town today, either in late afternoon or early evening. Suppertime would be a good time when everybody was off the streets.

The three riding behind him dropped farther behind and began to talk among themselves. They kept their voices low and Dan couldn't understand what they said. He turned his head once and looked at them. Elmer Tinker had his hand on his rifle, as though he was about to slip it out of the saddle scabbard at his side.

Dan felt irritable and angry. He halted his horse and swung him around. He said furiously, 'Damn it, I've had about all I'm going to put up with from you and from the

132

rest of the people back there in town. Either you ride along with me and help me splice the wire or turn around and go back. But don't keep muttering like a goddam bunch of old women!'

They looked at him sullenly. He went on angrily, 'Smead went out a while ago to try and get some men who were willing to defend the town. Know how many of you he got?' He gave them an instant to answer but nobody said anything. 'I'll tell you how many he got. He got none. Not a damn one of you was willing to fight for what's yours. So don't grumble about me or I might lose my temper and kick the hell out of a few of you. At least I'm going to be up over the bank with a rifle when they come riding in. And it's my kinfolk that I'm going to be shooting at!'

He didn't wait for a reply. He whirled his horse and sank the spurs. He thundered along the railroad right of way beside the telegraph poles, looking up at each span of wire as he rode to be sure it was intact.

He had gone four or five miles before he found the place where it had been cut. One cut end laid on the ground, the other dangled from a pole.

He dismounted and tied his horse. He sat down on the ground and began to put the climbers on.

The three who had accompanied him rode up and sat their horses, looking down at him.

He stuck a pair of pliers in his pocket, hung the loop of wire over his shoulder, adjusted the safety belt on the pole and began to climb.

Sullenly the three watched him. When he was up on the pole, he lowered an end of the wire loop and told one of them to tie the dangling wire onto it. He pulled it up, scraped the ends and, after touching them together a dozen times so that the telegrapher back in Dobeville would get the signal on his instrument, he spliced them together and climbed back down the pole. He untied his horse, mounted, and rode back toward town, not even looking back to see if the others were following.

CHAPTER SIXTEEN

When Dan and the other three arrived back in town, the streets were deserted. Dan stopped at the depot to drop off the tools. He yelled at Gus Shipley to come out and when Gus opened the station door Dan asked, 'Did you get that message off to Fort Dodge all right?'

Shipley nodded. 'The troops are leaving on the morning train, but they can't get here until late afternoon.'

Dan nodded. 'Where is everybody?'

'Over at the church. There's a town meeting going on.'

134

Dan looked at the three who had accompanied him. 'Go ahead up to the meeting if you want. I don't need you any more.'

They rode up Main, heading for the church. Dan followed more slowly. He stopped at the jail and tried the door. It was locked. He unlocked it and went inside. He opened the door leading to the cells and looked in at Jennie and at Flood. He didn't speak to either of them, nor did he give them a chance to speak to him. He closed the door, went back out, and relocked the outside door.

Smead would probably prefer that he stay away from the meeting but he didn't intend doing so. He wasn't going to hide out from the people of Dobeville. If they had anything to say about him, he would prefer they said it to his face.

He mounted his horse and rode up Main. At the bank, he turned left and rode over to Grape. The church was half a block above Fourth Street on Grape.

There were a few saddle horses and buggies in front of the church, but most of the people had come on foot. Dan tied his horse and went up the walk to the door. He opened it and stepped inside.

The church was full to overflowing. At the rear, by the door, men were standing five or six deep. Dan could see over their heads. Up front, where the altar was, there were about a dozen men, those who were the most prominent in the town. There were Charles Amherst, the Methodist minister, Ian Smitherman, Hans Overstreet, Larry Widemeier, Ralph Morris, and Doc Sinclair. Luke Smead was there, as were Harry Cooper, John Temple, and Ev Mason.

Luke Smead had the floor and Frank Delaney, standing in the front row, was yelling something at him. There was so much noise in the room that Dan couldn't make out what Frank was trying to say.

Smead raised both hands and yelled, 'Shut up! Quiet! How can we decide anything if everybody talks at once?'

Someone howled, 'What's to decide? You say the Youngerman gang is coming to raid the bank! You say if we fight them, they'll set fire to the town! Then I say we'd better not try fighting them!'

A score of voices yelled agreement, and the bedlam drowned out the one who had yelled first.

Smead shouted, 'And what about the bank? You may save your homes, but the bank will be busted. Every one of you who has money in it will lose it.'

'That'll be better than seeing them burn the whole damn town.'

Amherst raised a protesting voice at the use of profanity in the church. He was shouted down.

Smead roared, 'Letting them have the money in the bank doesn't mean they won't burn the town. Frank here killed a member of the gang. We have another member down there in jail. A third was pistol-whipped by Dan Youngerman yesterday.'

He suddenly saw Dan standing at the rear door. He beckoned. 'Come on up here, Dan!'

Dan pushed through the crowd, trying to work his way down the aisle. A few voices raised in resentment at being pushed. A couple of men pushed back. They closed ranks in front of him and Smead yelled angrily, 'Let him through!'

Dan began to fight his way through. He swept one man aside with his arm. He elbowed another in the ribs and roughly pushed a third ahead of him down the aisle.. He was thoroughly angry and perhaps the fact that he was, opened a path through those who still blocked his way. He strode down the aisle toward the front of the church.

Smead asked, 'Get the line fixed, Dan?'

Dan nodded.

'Did Gus get the message through?'

Again Dan nodded. 'The troops will leave tomorrow morning on the first train out of Dodge. They'll be here by late afternoon.'

Smead raised both hands to quiet the crowd. 'Dan says he and the others found the break in the telegraph line. They spliced it and Gus got the message through to Dodge. Troops will leave on the morning train and will be here tomorrow afternoon.'

Frank Delaney yelled drunkenly, 'That ain't gonna help! The Youngerman gang will be thirty-forty miles away by tomorrow afternoon. The town will be a pile of ashes.'

Smead raised his hands again. His face was red. He looked harried and worried, and he was obviously angry and disgusted with the attitudes of the people inside the church.

The crowd quieted briefly and Smead yelled, 'We can defend the town. We can wipe out the Wilkes-Youngerman gang once and for all. All I need is about ten men who think their homes and families are worth fighting for.'

Doc Sinclair stepped up beside Smead. He also raised his hands to calm the crowd. He yelled, 'It's not as simple as the sheriff tries to make it sound! The Wilkes-Youngerman gang is as vicious as Quantrill's bunch ever was! If they're balked, they'll not only burn the town, they'll kill everybody that stands in their way. They'll likely rape every woman that takes their fancy. And they'll get the money in the bank anyhow.'

'What do *you* think we ought to do?'

'I think we'd better get ready to fight the fires if and wherever they are set. Get buckets and get all the water ready that you can. Let the Youngerman gang have the money in the bank.'

Smead said, 'Shut up, Doc!' At the crowd he

138

yelled, 'Don't listen to him!'

Doc turned to face the sheriff, his neck turning red. 'Don't you try to shut me up! I have as much right . . .'

The sheriff raised both his hands again. 'Ten men! That's all I need! Aren't there ten men here who can shoot a gun and who have the guts to fight to save their homes?'

The bedlam quieted temporarily. A lot of the men in the room looked guiltily at the floor. But no voices raised. Les Porter, the gunsmith, started to shout something but his wife, standing beside him, caught his arm and prevented him.

Doc Sinclair yelled, 'I don't know about the rest of you, but I'm going to get out of town. I don't own anything that's worth getting killed about.'

The doors of the church opened at the back of the room. People began to crowd toward them, began to push into the street. Smead looked at Dan, shaking his head with plain disgust. He growled, 'Ten men. That's all I asked for. You'd think there'd be ten men with the guts to fight for what's right in a town this size.'

Delaney was sitting in the front pew. His face was red from shouting. He took a whisky bottle from his pocket, pulled the cork, and tipped the bottle up. Dan said, 'Put that away. This is a church.'

Delaney got to his feet. He stood there

weaving, staring belligerently at Dan. 'Who are you to tell me what to do? You're one of 'em. You probably brought 'em here.' He started to tip up the bottle again. Dan stepped forward and knocked it out of his hand. It crashed to the floor and its contents gurgled out.

Dan's action had been unthinking and he knew he had acted from anger, frustration, and disillusionment. But it was done.

Delaney dived for the bottle and recovered it before all of its contents had drained out on the floor. He turned and glared at Dan. He took another drink defiantly, then turned his head and yelled at the departing crowd, 'We got us a Youngerman right here in town! I say let's string him up! Maybe the rest of you believe that story that he ain't one of 'em, but by God I don't!'

The sheriff stepped between Dan and Frank. 'Shut up, Frank. We've got enough trouble without you stirring up some more.'

'I will not shut up an' you can't shut me up! I know my rights!' He tilted the bottle again.

Smead said, 'I thought you were going to get out of town.'

'I am. When I'm ready to go.'

'I gave you the money to get out of town. What'd you do with it?'

'I still got it. I got enough, anyhow.' Delaney turned his head and bawled at the last of the departing crowd, 'What you goin' to do about Dan Youngerman? You goin' to let him get away with what he's done?' He tilted up the bottle again, draining the last few drops. He looked down at it a moment, then turned and hurled it at Dan. Dan ducked and the bottle smashed against the wall.

He stepped forward. Delaney saw him coming and grabbed for his gun. Dan reached him as his hand touched its grips. He twisted Delaney's arm behind him, forcing it high against his shoulder blades. With his left hand he held Delaney thus, while with his right he removed the man's gun from its holster and tossed it to Smead. He said, 'All right, Frank. You can sober up in jail.'

The bluster was suddenly gone from Frank. The blood drained out of his face. 'You can't do that! You can't do that to me! That gang will kill me when they come!'

'You should have thought of that before.'

Delaney looked at Smead. 'Sheriff?'

Smead shook his head. 'I gave you a chance to get out of town. I even gave you the money.'

'I'll go! I swear I'll go this time! Please, sheriff. Oh God, please let me go!'

Smead said, 'Take him down and lock him up.'

Dan pushed Delaney up the aisle, still holding his arm high against his shoulder blades.

Cooper and Winslow had remained in the church but everybody else had gone. Cooper looked at Smead. 'Where do you want us,

Luke?'

'Come on down to the jail with us. I'll give you both guns and tell you where to station yourselves.'

Dan and Delaney stepped out into the sunlight. Smead, Cooper, and Winslow followed them. Smead said, 'Go on down to the jail. One of you take Dan's horse with you. I'm going to stop at the hotel and get meals for the prisoners.'

Without releasing Delaney's arm, Dan pushed the drunken man ahead of him down the street. Delaney staggered a little but since each stagger brought greater pain to his twisted arm, he soon managed to control his staggering. Dan smiled grimly to himself. There could be no doubt that Delaney was drunk but he wasn't nearly as drunk as he wanted people to think he was.

The streets were virtually deserted now. All the townspeople had scattered to their homes. Dan wondered what they would do. Would they stay in town and fight the fires the gang set wherever they broke out? Or would they run, taking what valuables they could and leaving the rest behind?

It was well past noon and he was hungry now himself. His breakfast had been early and he'd been pretty busy since.

Main Street was as deserted as the other streets had been. Dan wondered if Sam realized how badly this town was demoralized.

He now had little hope that Sam and the rest of the gang could be fought off successfully. He and Smead and Cooper and Winslow would do what they could, but it wasn't going to be enough. They'd hurt Sam just enough to enrage him, just enough to make him strike back savagely at the town. He'd leave it burning. He would probably succeed in killing most, if not all, of the four defending it.

He might even take Sarah and the children with him when he left. Dan's jawline tightened as he clenched his jaws. There had to be something they could do! They were forewarned and there had to be something they could do!

He reached the jail. Without releasing Delaney, he unlocked the door and opened it. He pushed Frank across the room and through the door leading to the cells. Just outside the empty cell, Delaney put up a brief struggle, but Dan's inexorable grip on his arm stopped his struggle immediately. A cry of pain escaped Delaney's lips.

Dan released him and shoved him roughly into the cell. He slammed and locked the door.

Jennie was staring at him triumphantly. 'You'd better run while you still can.'

He didn't bother to reply. She looked at Delaney from behind her screen. He hoped Delaney would keep his mouth shut about killing Hugh. Jennie had no way of knowing who he was if he didn't tell her himself.

He returned to the office. Cooper and Ned Winslow were staring out into the street. They both looked scared. He wondered if they were going to go back on their promise to help him and Smead defend the town. He suddenly found himself wishing that Sam would come and have it over with. Nothing could be worse than this endless waiting for him to come.

CHAPTER SEVENTEEN

Cooper and Winslow sat glumly, staring at the floor. Dan paced irritably back and forth. Half an hour passed but, at last, Dan saw the sheriff and hurried to open the door for him.

Carrying three covered trays stacked up, the sheriff came into the jail. Dan took the trays from him and put them down. The smell of food made him feel sick at his stomach, but he supposed that was only nerves.

One by one, he carried the trays back into the cell block and gave them to the prisoners. Jennie didn't get up from her cot, so Dan left the tray on the floor inside her cell door. Flood glowered at him, but he came to the door, picked up his tray and carried it back to the bunk. He sat down and began to eat. Delaney didn't even look up. He only said weakly, 'Get that out of here. I'm sick enough as it is.'

Dan withdrew carrying the tray. He returned to the office with it. 'Delaney doesn't want his. He's too sick.'

Smead said, 'Then I'll eat it.' He looked at Cooper and at Winslow. 'You two had better go get something to eat. Come back as soon as you can and we'll get set.'

The two went out. Smead, chewing a bite of roast beef, glanced up at Dan. 'Think they'll come back?'

Dan shrugged. 'I wouldn't blame 'em much if they didn't.'

'Go get yourself something to eat.'

Dan nodded. 'I'll hurry.'

Smead did not reply. Dan went out into the street. He glanced up and down its length but Cooper and Winslow were the only two he saw. He untied his horse, mounted, and trotted the animal swiftly up the street.

At the corner in front of the bank, he glanced again at the various vantage points he had selected earlier. It didn't look as if they were going to get the men they had to have. At the moment, he wasn't even sure Cooper and Winslow would return.

And if they did not, what would he do? There was really only one thing he could do. He'd have to shoot Sam himself, hoping that, deprived of their leader, the gang would quit.

The thought of killing his own brother made him feel empty inside. The ties of family were as strong in him as they were in Sam, but,

145

unlike Sam, he would be trying to save the lives and property of these people who had become such a large part of his life. He would be doing what was right.

He turned up Elm Street and headed toward his house. In front of the house next door a wagon was drawn up, and his neighbors, the Murphys, were carrying things out and loading them. Link Murphy ducked his head and refused to look at Dan. Dan didn't speak. He tied his horse in front of his own house and went up the walk. He opened the door and went inside.

Sarah was there. The children were playing upstairs. He could hear their running footsteps on the floor overhead.

Sarah's face was drawn and pale. 'The Murphys are leaving, Dan.'

'I know. I saw them loading up.'

'When do you think Sam will come?'

'Probably late this afternoon. He knows by now that Jennie isn't coming back, and he's probably guessed that we've thrown her in jail.'

'Did you get enough men to fight him off?'

He laughed bitterly. 'We got two, Cooper and Winslow, and neither one of us is sure they won't back out. They've gone to eat right now and they may not bother to come back.'

'And if they don't?'

'Then Smead and I will have to do as much as possible by ourselves.'

'Dan, that's suicide. You can't do it. I won't

let you.'

He said, 'You'll let me because it's what I have to do. It's my job and Luke's and we'll do it no matter what. Maybe when the chips are down, the townspeople will pitch in and help.'

'You know better, Dan.'

'I suppose so.'

'I'm going to come down and help you. I can shoot . . .'

He said firmly, 'You're going to do your job just like I'm trying to do mine. The children are your responsibility and you're going to take care of them.'

Her glance held his for a long time. She ran to him suddenly, sobbing, and his arms closed tight around her. He held her thus for a while but at last he said, 'Sarah, I have to get back. Can you fix me something to eat?'

She drew back, wiping her tears away with the back of her hand. She hurried to the kitchen as though grateful for something to do that would keep her hands busy and calm her thoughts. He heard a pan bang against the stove and heard the sound of dishes being withdrawn from the cupboard.

He went into the kitchen after her. He sat down wearily at the kitchen table. It had been a busy morning. The worry had been as bad as the activity, he thought. And the hostility of the townspeople toward him was hardest of all to bear.

Sarah, pausing at the back door a moment,

said, 'Dan, look.'

Dan got up and went to the door. Across the alley, the Reed family was loading personal possessions into their buggy, which was drawn up at their back gate.

Sarah asked, 'Do you suppose everybody is leaving town?'

Dan shrugged. It angered him that the townspeople were running out on their responsibilities, It angered him that they were so ready to condemn him, yet so willing to let him and Luke Smead take the brunt of what was happening.

He returned to the table and sat down again. 'Sarah. My dinner. I have to get back downtown.'

'I'm sorry.' She returned to the stove.

Dan said, 'If Sam and the others come, and if they set fire to the town, I want you to get away with the children. I want you to promise me you will. I don't want to have to worry about whether the three of you are safe.'

'Dan, I . . .'

He stared steadily at her and at last she nodded reluctantly. 'All right, Dan. I promise.'

He waited with seeming patience. Inside he was seething with anxiety. Sarah put his dinner before him and he ate it as quickly as he could. He gulped the last of the coffee. Then he took the stairway two steps at a time and went into the room where the children were.

Both came running to him when they saw

148

him and he knelt and gathered them into his arms. He wondered if this was the last time he'd see them. He supposed it was. He didn't have much hope that either he or the sheriff could survive.

He said, 'I'll be late coming home tonight, kids, so you go to bed when your mother tells you to.'

He didn't know whether they heard or not, because both of them were trying to talk to him. Grinning, he rumpled their hair briefly, then rose and went back downstairs.

He took Sarah into his arms and kissed her. She was sobbing openly when he released her. He turned and bolted from the house.

The anger that had stirred in him off and on over the past few days, was now a steady thing that would neither diminish nor go away. Sam and the gang might kill him. They might also kill Luke Smead, and Cooper, and Winslow. They might burn the town. But Dan promised himself one thing. He would hurt the gang. He would kill as many of them as he could. He and Smead could cripple the Wilkes-Youngerman gang so badly it would never be a threat to anyone again. They might be members of Dan's family but in coming here they were attacking him. It could be no mortal sin to defend himself, his wife and children, and his neighbors and friends.

He untied his horse, mounted, and rode down the street. When he reached Main, he saw four loaded wagons creaking along it toward the lower end of town. Children sat atop the loads. Parents sat grimly on the wagon seats. The wagons were loaded with hastily chosen valuables, with household goods, with the things the occupants would need to survive until the Youngerman gang had come and gone.

He turned his horse down Main toward the jail. Except for the wagons, the street was deserted. Panic had touched the town and this exodus would only serve to increase it. The panic would snowball, with more and more families leaving until the town was virtually without inhabitants.

He stopped in front of the Kansas Hotel. Turning into Main from Fourth Street was a cavalcade of assorted conveyances. Leading were half a dozen horsemen. Following were buckboards, buggies, wagons, even an ancient two-wheel cart.

Dan reined his horse out into the middle of the street. He didn't know if he was going to be able to stop anybody from leaving town, but he knew he had to try. When the leading horsemen stopped, he said, 'You're doing exactly what they want you to. You're turning the bank and the town over to them without a fight.'

A man named Hal Banks spoke for the group. Heavy and middle-aged, he worked for Sol Silverman in the Dobeville Mercantile. He said, 'Get out of our way, deputy, and don't preach to us. You brought this trouble here. You and your outlaw family have what you want but don't be here when we get back. Just don't be here then.'

Dan's smoldering anger flared. 'Don't tell me what to do, Mr. Banks. I'm staying and you're running away. If Smead had the six of you to station around the bank, we could beat the Youngerman gang.'

'Sure. Maybe so. But how many of us would be dead afterward? And what would be left of our town?'

'There's not going to be much left of it if you run away.'

Back in the cavalcade of wagons and buckboards, a woman began to screech imprecations at Dan. One of the men turned his head and said sternly, 'Bessie, be still.'

She continued to shriek, and the man roared, 'Bessie!'

She was silent after that. Banks said, 'Get out of the way, deputy.'

Dan shook his head. 'Go back,' he pleaded. 'Stay in town and help the sheriff and me defend it.'

Banks's horse moved forward. So did the horses of the other five. The wagons, buggies, and buckboards creaked into motion behind them.

There was no use in further argument. These people were scared and angry, and they blamed him for their predicament. Dan pulled back and watched them as they continued down the street. He did not move again until their wagons and buckboards had rattled across the railroad tracks and headed out into the open prairie beyond.

CHAPTER EIGHTEEN

Smead had finished eating. He was standing at the window, staring into the street. His face seemed haggard and there was a bleak look in his eyes.

Dan suddenly felt terribly ashamed. He had brought this trouble to Dobeville. Sam and the gang were coming because of him. And Smead would die because they were coming here.

He closed the door behind him. He looked at the sheriff and said, 'It doesn't sound like enough, but I'm sorry, Luke. I'd do anything to change the way things are but I don't know what to do.'

Smead turned his head and gave a humorless smile. 'You can stay and fight it out with me. That's what you were hired for and that's what I expect of you.'

'Do you think we can get anybody else?'

Smead shook his head. 'I doubt it. We can keep trying, but we don't have much time.'

'How about Delaney? Maybe he'd rather

152

fight than lay back there in jail. He knows they'll be coming here after Jennie, and he knows they'll kill him when they do.'

'Go ask him.'

Dan went out in back. He looked into Delaney's cell. The man lay on the cot, his eyes closed. Dan asked, 'Want to help us fight 'em off?'

Delaney opened his eyes and turned his head. 'Have I got a choice?'

'Sure. You can stay here if you don't want to fight.'

'And when they come they'll kill me.'

'Probably.' Dan hesitated a moment. Then he added, 'If they find out you were the one who killed Hugh Wilkes.'

Delaney sat up, his face pale. 'For God's sake, shut up! That damned woman will hear . . .'

Dan tried to look startled. He had deliberately let slip the fact that Delaney had killed Hugh Wilkes. He had just suddenly gotten to figuring that Delaney *ought* to help. Sam Youngerman was going to exact vengeance on Dobeville for the death of Wilkes, and since Delaney was responsible for that, he owed it to the town to help fight off the gang.

Delaney was staring at him suspiciously. 'You let that slip out on purpose, didn't you?'

'Maybe. We need help. We need it bad.'

Delaney came across to the door. 'All right.

153

Let me out. You didn't leave me much choice when you let her know it was me that killed Wilkes.'

Dan asked, 'Have I got your word that you won't run out on us?'

Delaney nodded sourly. He held out his hands. They were shaking violently. 'I don't know how much good I'll be though, shaking like I am.'

'You'll be all right. We'll give you a shotgun and load it with buck.'

He unlocked the cell door and Delaney came out. Flood asked, 'Don't I get the same deal as him?'

Dan shook his head.

'Why not? What the hell you got against me?'

Dan said, 'I don't trust you.'

Flood began to curse. Dan ignored him and went into the office, following Delaney. He closed the door behind him. He looked at Smead. 'You don't want to try trusting Flood to help us, do you?'

Smead shook his head.

Dan said, 'I think we'd better go up there to the bank and get set.'

Smead grunted, 'Doesn't look much like Cooper and Winslow are coming back.' He went to the gunrack and unlocked the chain that ran through the trigger guards of the guns. He glanced at Dan. 'What kind of gun do you want?'

154

'I want two. I want a rifle and a double-barreled shotgun.'

Smead handed him two guns. Delaney said, 'Just a shotgun for me. I'm too shaky for a rifle.'

Smead gave him a shotgun. He got a rifle and shotgun for himself, then opened a drawer in his desk. He gave both Delaney and Dan a box of shotgun shells, and gave Dan a box of rifle shells for the Spencer carbine. He got some shells for himself, emptying the shotgun shells into the right-hand pocket of his coat, the carbine shells into the left.

Dan crossed the room and opened the door. He felt a vast relief when he saw Cooper and Winslow approaching from the direction of the bank. Cooper grinned ruefully. 'I have to admit, it was a temptation, Dan. With everybody else leaving town, it was a temptation to go along with them. If they don't care about either their bank or their town, then why should we?'

Dan grinned back. 'I'm glad you do, though. Come on in and the sheriff will give you some guns.'

Smead issued a rifle and shotgun to each of the two men. Then, carrying their armament, the five walked toward the intersection of Fourth and Main.

Glancing at his watch, Dan saw that it was almost four o'clock. A couple of wagons passed, heading east along Fourth. Smead

155

asked, 'Any preference, gentlemen?'

Cooper said, 'I think Ned and I would like to be over the bank, if it's all the same to you.'

Smead looked at Dan. 'Any objection to that?'

Dan shook his head. 'I guess not, but I think they've picked the most dangerous place to be.' He looked at Cooper. 'Why don't you reconsider, Mr. Cooper? The old Booth Hotel will give you better cover because those brick walls will stop a bullet.'

Cooper glanced at the vacant hotel. He nodded reluctantly. 'I suppose you're right.'

Dan pointed to one of the boarded-up windows facing Main. He pointed to another window that faced Fourth. 'If you'll station yourselves in those two windows, you'll be all set.'

They started away. Dan said, 'Wait a minute.'

They turned their heads and looked at him. Dan said, 'Sam Youngerman is my brother but he's plenty mean and so are the others. Don't shoot to wound any of them. Shoot to kill. They're as dangerous wounded as any wild animal.'

Cooper stared at him strangely for a moment. Then he nodded and followed Winslow toward the entrance of the hotel. He broke the door glass with his rifle butt, then reached in and unbolted the door. He and Winslow disappeared inside.

Smead was staring at Dan, and Dan realized the sheriff intended to let him decide where everybody was to be stationed. Dan said, 'I'll take the windows over the bank. Luke, I think you ought to be in that passageway. Delaney, why don't you get on the roof of the Abstract Company, behind that high false front. It's high enough so that you can rest your shotgun on it, and if you keep changing position, they probably won't be able to get you through the wood.'

Delaney agreed. Dan said, 'It's going to be a long wait, Frank. Think you can stay awake?'

Delaney nodded but it was plain to Dan that he was not too sure he could. Dan said, 'You can climb up in back. There's a cottonwood branch that hangs out over the roof.'

Delaney headed up Fourth toward the rear of the Abstract Company office. Dan looked at the sheriff. Smead nodded faintly at him, then turned and headed for the passageway between Smitherman's and the corner building next to it. Dan climbed the outside stairway on the north side of the bank and opened the door at the top.

There was a short hallway with two doors, one leading to the office of Doc Sinclair, the other to Ralph Morris's office. Dan tried the door of Doc's office and found it locked. The door to Morris's office was also locked. He hesitated a moment, then stepped away and lashed out with a flat-footed kick about doorknob high.

The door held. Dan kicked again, harder this time, and the door flew open, to crash back against the wall. He went in.

He crossed to the window, unlocked and raised it. He removed the screen and set it aside. He leaned out.

He could see Cooper in one of the windows of the Booth Hotel, one of those facing Fourth. He couldn't see Ned Winslow, who would be in one of the windows facing Main. Smead was visible in the passageway on the other side of the intersection, and Frank Delaney's head was visible over the false front of the Booth County Abstract Company.

Dan turned. He got Ralph Morris's leather-covered swivel chair and rolled it over to the window. He sat down wearily. He leaned the shotgun against the wall within easy reach, then found and packed his pipe. He lighted it.

It must be close to five o'clock, he thought, which meant there were around three hours of daylight left. He doubted if Sam would try to raid the bank after dark. Darkness could hide too many ambushes.

He stared down into the street, a slight frown on his face. It was now deserted except for a single, heavily loaded wagon rattling hurriedly across the railroad tracks at the lower end of Main.

He wondered how many of the townspeople had pulled out of town. More than half, he

158

supposed. He hadn't counted the wagons and other conveyances leaving, but there had to have been fifty, at the very least.

Sam couldn't fail to see how many had pulled out. He would meet some of them on the road. He might question those he met and if he did, he would know how defenseless the town really was.

He would also know Dan and the sheriff were waiting for him. He might find out about Cooper and Winslow. He'd surely learn that Jennie was being held in jail.

The frown on Dan's face deepened. Sam didn't like ambushes, even when they were as lightly manned as this one was. He hadn't kept the gang intact by riding into ambushes. So it was virtually certain that he would fire the town as he rode in. He'd hold back long enough afterward for the people to discover the fires and run to put them out. It was then that he'd hit the bank.

Dan held his hands up in front of his face. They were still trembling, but not as badly as they had been trembling a while ago. They had steadied and he was steadier inside as well. He could fire down into the gang when they rode in. He thought he could shoot to kill, particularly if they had left plumes of smoke rising behind them as they rode into town.

The shadows lengthened in the street. An hour dragged past. Dan occasionally leaned out of the window to check on the other men.

159

Delaney had apparently gone to sleep. Dan hadn't seen him for more than half an hour now. He hoped that when the gang rode in, the shots would waken Delaney in time for him to be of use.

Another hour dragged slowly past. The clouds flamed orange from the setting sun. Dan was hungry now, and irritable as well. But he knew exactly what was in Sam's mind. Sam was taking full advantage of the terror his anticipated coming had inspired in the inhabitants of Dobeville. He knew that if he waited until morning, most of those still remaining would follow those who had already left.

Cooper and Delaney and Winslow had manned their posts this afternoon. But would they be able to stand the strain of waiting throughout the night? Dan didn't think they would.

Sam figured everyone would run out on the sheriff and his deputy. And the hell of it was, everyone probably would.

CHAPTER NINETEEN

Light gradually faded from the evening sky. A few stars winked out.

Main Street was an almost eerie sight tonight. Not a single light burned anywhere along its length. Once, Dan saw a match flare on the roof of the Booth County Abstract Company as Delaney lighted up a smoke.

An hour after complete darkness had fallen, Smead came out of the passageway and stood beneath the bank windows to call, 'Dan?'

'Yeah?'

'We've got to eat. Do you suppose there's any kitchen help at the Kansas Hotel?'

'I can go see.'

'Do that. I doubt if that bunch will come tonight. We'll stay on the job but I think that after we eat, most of the men had just as well try and get some sleep.'

Dan leaned rifle and shotgun against the wall beside the window and groped his way to the door. Outside on the landing, the stars made enough light for him to see the steps. The moon had not yet come up. He descended and walked down the street to the Kansas Hotel.

It was dark inside and the door was locked. He returned to the bank intersection and called out for Smead. The sheriff answered him.

Dan said, 'The hotel's locked up tighter than a drum. I told Sarah to take the children and leave, but maybe she hasn't gone. I could go see if she could cook something up for us.'

'All right.'

Dan walked along Fourth toward home. There was a lamp burning in the kitchen. He

161

called out before he stepped onto the porch because he didn't want to frighten her.

The kitchen was warm and there was a fire in the stove. He could smell coffee. Sarah looked at him with plain relief showing in her eyes. 'Dan, do you suppose it was all a bluff? Is it possible that Sam and the others won't even come?'

He shook his head. 'They'll come, in the morning. Where are the kids?'

She glanced at him guiltily. 'I sent them away with Agnes Nelson. She'll take good care of them. I know she will.'

'I wanted you with them. I wanted to know that *you* were safe.'

'I'll be safe here, Dan. Sam wouldn't hurt me and neither would the others. You don't have to worry about me.'

'You're to stay right here in this house. Do you understand?'

She nodded meekly. 'Yes, Dan.'

He continued to study her doubtfully as he said, 'The hotel is locked up tight and we need something to eat. There are five of us. Can you fix something?'

'Of course. I'll have it ready in half an hour.'

'I'll come back then and pick it up.'

He stared worriedly at her for a moment. Then he turned and went back into the darkness. He had no faith that she would do what he had told her to. She had sent the children away instead of taking them. When the shooting started tomorrow, he couldn't be sure she wouldn't get a gun herself and take part in the town's defense. But he couldn't lock her up. There was nothing he could do but hope she'd stay out of it.

He hurried back to the bank. Smead was squatted comfortably against the wall. He was smoking a cigar. Dan hunkered down beside him. 'I was right. She hadn't left. She sent the kids away with Agnes Nelson. She'll fix something and have it ready in half an hour.'

'Go tell Delaney. I'll yell up to Cooper and Winslow.'

Dan crossed the street to the building that housed the Abstract Company. He called up, 'Frank?'

There was no answer. He called again, louder this time. Still there was no answer. He went back to where the tree was that grew out over the roof.

He climbed to the top of the fence and from there up an overhanging branch until he could drop down onto the roof. He went toward the front of the roof where the false front was. Again he called, 'Frank?'

Delaney wasn't there. He searched the entire roof without finding him.

Disgustedly, he returned to the rear of the roof and started to reach for the tree. A scuffing noise below drew his attention. He put a hand on the grips of his gun.

But it was only Delaney coming up the tree.

Delaney dropped to the roof. It was too dark for Dan to see his expression, but he drew in his breath with startled surprise. Dan said, 'Where the hell have you been? You said you'd . . .'

'I didn't run out on you. I came back, didn't I?'

Dan caught the reek of whisky on his breath. He said, 'Give me the bottle, damn it. I'll have some food down here for you in half an hour.'

'Ah hell, Dan, a few drinks ain't going to hurt.'

'Give me the bottle. I want you awake when they come, not passed out cold. If you can't lay off the bottle for this one night, then I'll just put you back in jail.'

Delaney reluctantly handed the bottle to him. Dan threw it off the roof and heard it shatter on the ground in the back yard of the Abstract Company.

He said sourly, 'Get on the job and stay on it.'

He climbed back to the ground. For a moment he stood there in the darkness disgustedly. Out of this whole town, he and Smead had been able to get only three to help. And one of the three was handicapped with a hangover and a thirst and would have to be watched every minute of the time.

It had been nearly half an hour since he left Sarah. He returned along Fourth and up the alley behind the house.

164

The food was almost ready. Dan sat down and drank a cup of coffee while she finished. She had a big pot of stew, a pot of coffee, and a couple of loaves of bread. She said, 'I'll have to help you carry it.'

'All right. Provided you come right back.'

She agreed. Dan carried the coffee and the stew and Sarah brought the other things, bread, plates, silverware, cups. They groped their way along the pitch-black street to the intersection of Fourth and Main. Dan put the food down in front of the bank. He called to Smead and the sheriff came out of the darkness.

Dan kissed Sarah lightly on the mouth. 'Go on home now and get some sleep.'

'You don't seriously think I could sleep tonight?'

'It won't hurt to try. Nothing's going to happen before morning.'

She disappeared into the darkness, too willingly he thought. Smead got himself a plate of stew and some bread and coffee and sat down to eat. Dan followed suit. When he had finished, he carried a plate and cup over to Delaney and called him down off the roof. Smead called to Cooper and Winslow similarly.

Afterward, Dan took the first lookout and the others stretched out where they were and tried to go to sleep.

He had no trouble staying awake. He was

165

nervous and tense. For a while he paced restlessly back and forth in Morris's office above the bank. Every now and then he would go to the window, lean out, and peer into the darkness even though he knew Sam would never come at night.

Near midnight, he descended the stairs into the street. He had intended calling Smead to take the next watch, but he found the sheriff sitting comfortably with his back against the front wall of Smitherman's, sound asleep. The sheriff was snoring softly.

Dan didn't disturb him. He couldn't sleep himself anyway so there didn't seem to be much point. Instead, he crossed to the Abstract Company office and climbed the tree to the roof. In the moonlight, he could see Delaney stretched out full length on the roof. He didn't disturb him but climbed back down the tree. As he headed for the stairway at the side of the bank, Cooper called from the window of the old Booth Hotel, 'Everything all right?'

'Uh huh. What's the matter, can't you sleep?'

'Nope. Want me to take over the lookout so you can sleep?'

Dan said, 'No, I wouldn't be able to sleep either.'

Cooper was silent and Dan turned away. He climbed to the second story of the bank and sat down in front of the window to wait. There was nothing else that he could do. But in his mind he could see Sam and the other members of the gang, perhaps even now approaching the town, holding their horses to a steady, tireless walk.

*   *   *

Sarah went home immediately when she left Dan. She took the lamp from the kitchen table and went upstairs. She found Dan's double-barreled shotgun in the upstairs closet. She also found a couple of boxes of shells, which were filled with bird shot. She found one filled with buck.

Frowning, she carried shotgun and shells downstairs. Maybe she couldn't kill anyone with shells filled with bird shot, but at twenty or thirty feet she could hurt them. She could distract them and she might save Dan's life.

Sarah knew something Dan did not. She knew he would never be able to shoot at Sam and his other brothers in the street. He might think he could if the pressure was great enough but he was wrong. Sarah knew how strong family loyalties were among the members of Dan's family.

No such scruples would bother her. She blew out the lamp and went out, closing the door behind her. The night air was chilly and she discovered she was shivering. She wished she had brought a sweater, but she didn't go back for one.

167

Silently, she walked along Fourth. She didn't know where to hide herself so that Dan wouldn't see her when it got light. She finally settled on the vacant lot next to the bank. If she stayed concealed behind the north wall of the bank, none of the men waiting for the gang would see her until it was too late.

She sat down and put her back against the wall of the bank. The weeds rustled slightly as she did. She laid the shotgun and shells down on the ground at her feet, then raised her knees and hugged them against herself with her arms. She discovered that doing so kept her from feeling quite so cold.

She closed her eyes and tried to go to sleep, but sleep wouldn't come. Wide awake, she waited for the dawn.

CHAPTER TWENTY

Dawn began as a faint lightening of the sky in the east. It made a line where the dark silhouette of rolling plain showed the contrast between earth and sky.

Cocks crowed all over town, in chicken coops behind nearly every house. A couple of dogs were barking and somewhere, a milch cow bawled, to be answered by her calf.

Morris's office had another window that faced on Fourth. Dan raised it and removed

168

the screen. He could see Cooper in the hotel window across the street. He could see Smead standing in front of Smitherman's, stretching out the stiffness of the night. Smead raised a hand and waved at him.

Dan looked along Fourth Street toward the east, leaning as far out of the window as he could. The far end of Fourth Street was hidden by the overhanging boughs of cottonwoods lining it, but he couldn't miss the sudden, dense column of smoke that billowed above them a hundred feet into the air. He turned his head and yelled, 'Sheriff! They've started a fire over at the east side of town.'

Smead yelled, 'Delaney! You awake?' and Dan heard Delaney shout a hoarse reply from behind the false front of the Booth County Abstract Company. Smead called, 'Winslow! Cooper! Are you awake?'

Both men yelled their replies. Smead shouted, 'Then get ready! They'll be here any minute now!'

Dan wondered whose house was burning behind the screening cottonwoods. He wondered if the owners were among those who had fled town yesterday.

He thought of Sarah and of his two children and he briefly hoped that Sarah would stay in the house. He knew her well enough to doubt it, but he also knew his brother Sam. Sam would have issued orders that Sarah was not to be harmed. Any member of the gang who

169

disregarded Sam's orders in this respect would die regretting it.

With the lightening sky, a breeze stirred in the east, blowing the column of smoke across the center of the town. Still the gang did not appear, but there could be no doubt that they were here.

Sam was taking no chances, Dan thought ruefully. He knew the town was forewarned. He knew there might be an ambush waiting for him.

He was reducing the odds as much as possible. He had fired something on the east side of town and the wind, which was freshening, would spread the fire inward toward the center of it. He probably had men on all sides of town right now, setting more fires in more houses. He meant to empty out the part of town where the bank was, if he could.

Dan returned to the window facing southwest into the intersection of Fourth and Main. Smead had moved into the middle of the intersection and was staring eastward at the rising smoke. Delaney's head and shoulders were visible over the false front of the building across the street.

Dan was in time to see a second plume of smoke rising down at the lower end of town where the depot was. And shortly thereafter, a third column raised almost directly west beyond the building that housed the Abstract

170

Company.

Men were shouting in the distance, their mingling shouts creating a strange, low, continuous sound though none of their words were distinguishable. Suddenly, from the vacant lot next to the livery barn, the town's fire engine came, drawn by its two teams. It thundered around the corner in front of the bank on two wheels, two men clinging precariously behind. Its bell clanged. Smoke from a hastily kindled fire beneath its boiler poured from its stack.

On all sides the fires were growing steadily. From the east, a pall of smoke drifted across the town. Dan could smell smoke now, wood smoke from a burning house or barn. Probably a house, he thought bitterly. Sam Youngerman wouldn't bother to set fire to outbuildings. That wouldn't terrify the people of Dobeville sufficiently.

Dan realized now that even if they had managed to recruit men to help them fight off the gang, the men would have deserted when they saw the fires burning in all parts of town. He glanced across at the old Booth Hotel. Cooper was still in the second-floor window. He couldn't see Winslow, but he supposed he was in the other window facing Main.

He leaned out and stared eastward along Fourth again. Smoke rolled along the street, pushed by a stiffening breeze out of the east. Out of that smoke came the Wilkes-

Youngerman gang, riding unhurriedly down the exact center of the street, by twos, like a troop of Confederate cavalry.

Leading them, riding alone, was Sam Youngerman. Staring down at Sam, it suddenly seemed to Dan as if the last seven years had not even passed. Sam looked exactly as he had seven years ago. He still had his full black beard. His black hair still curled on his thick, strong neck. He still wore the floppy, wide-brimmed gray hat, and while Dan knew it couldn't be the same one he wore when he rode with Quantrill during the war, it looked like it.

Hung diagonally across his chest, one from each shoulder, were full cartridge belts. Thrust into his belt were two pistols, one on each side. And in his hand was the rifle that he never went anywhere without.

Behind him rode Dan's uncle, Rufus Wilkes. Beside Rufus was Clem Youngerman, Dan's brother, a year younger than himself, and behind this pair were Win Youngerman and Hawkins, the man Dan had pistol-whipped and run out of town.

Smoke whirled around their heads, sometimes obscuring them temporarily. But always they came on, like the deadly horsemen of the Apocalypse, riding through the drifting clouds.

They were now less than a block away. Dan raised his glance and saw Cooper leaning out of his window staring fascinatedly at them. If Cooper opened up as they came in range, which was what he probably intended to do, he would draw their concentrated fire and be riddled before he even had a chance to duck. Dan yelled, 'Cooper!'

Cooper looked at him. Dan shouted, 'Hold your fire until you hear me shoot!'

He saw Cooper nod, saw the man withdraw into the shadows of the room so that he would not be so readily visible to members of the gang. Dan breathed a long sigh of relief. He wanted the gang to be all the way into the intersection before anybody began to shoot. He wanted all the defenders to have the gang in their sights, to open fire on them at once.

He now pulled back himself into the shadows of the room so that he could not be seen. But even from here, he would see the gang when they passed beneath his window. He would be able to count them and he would see them group in the intersection, defying the town's defenders to shoot at them.

Their arrogance was appalling, he thought angrily. They *knew* they had the people of this town terrified. He was suddenly reminded of a snake, hypnotizing a bird, able to devour it only because of the bird's paralyzing fear.

He wished he had fifty men stationed along this street. He wished he had enough men to cut this arrogant gang to bits and leave them lying scattered in the street.

Sam Youngerman rode past beneath his window, not even bothering to look up. Dan realized that his hands were trembling. 'Damn Sam! Damn him to hell!'

The others filed past by twos. Dan counted. There were thirteen men in all. More than he had counted on. And against those thirteen were five, one of them a terrified, shaky drunk.

They must all be in the intersection now. He went to the front window, the one facing diagonally into it.

Before he could raise the shotgun in his hands, a puff of smoke billowed from the wall beside the bank. The roar of a shotgun rolled across the street and echoed back instantly. Sam Youngerman's horse began to buck, and for once even the appallingly arrogant Sam had his hands full trying to keep his seat.

Someone else had found the courage to help defend the town. That was the thought that immediately crossed Dan's mind. And then suddenly he knew who was in the lot beside the bank. He knew, because Sam's horse was only stung. The shotgun beside the bank wall had been loaded with bird shot instead of buck. It was his own gun that he used for hunting, and Sarah had to have been the one who had fired it.

The gang swung their plunging horses, swung to face toward the lot beside the bank. In an instant . . .

Dan fired, not taking aim on any particular

174

target, shooting instead into the milling group. He had to distract them from Sarah, had to distract them immediately. Sam's orders that Sarah was not to be harmed weren't going to save her now.

Two more horses down there began to buck. A man toppled from his saddle. From the ground, he began to fire at Dan's window.

Smead's gun was firing from the passageway. Cooper began to shoot down from his window in the Booth Hotel. Dan couldn't see Winslow, but out of the corner of his eye he glimpsed a puff of smoke from the window where Winslow was. And across the street on the roof of the Abstract Company office, Delaney fired both barrels rapidly.

Out in the middle of the intersection a horse went down in a heap. Another made a shrill noise of pain that sounded almost human. A man fell limply from the saddle as his horse reared, and didn't move again.

Dan and the others had distracted them from Sarah, had even demoralized them momentarily, but now Sam's great roaring voice rallied them. They turned a deadly fire upward at the windows and the roof. Frank Delaney was literally riddled where he stood, by bullets tearing through the wood of the store's false front. He dropped his gun and it clattered to the boardwalk. He hung there in an upright position for an instant, staring unbelievingly at the horsemen milling around below in the intersection. Then he slipped downward and disappeared.

Bullets slammed into the flimsy frame walls of the bank's second story. One sent splinters flying into Dan's face. He could hear them ricocheting from the brick walls of the old hotel building across the street. He ducked back, broke the shotgun and reloaded it, then stepped to the window and fired again. This time he aimed at Hawkins who had a gun leveled toward the vacant lot beside the bank. He was gratified to see the man literally driven out of his saddle by the force of charge. Hawkins's horse thundered away in terror, but Hawkins lay motionless in the dust.

Cooper's gun was silent and so was Winslow's. Concentrated fire directed at the passageway where Smead had concealed himself had apparently forced him to withdraw. Dan realized suddenly that he was all alone. And now all the guns in the street below turned up toward him.

Suddenly he didn't care about the bank. He didn't even care whether Sam burned the town or not. All he could think of was Sarah, down there in the vacant lot beside the bank, perhaps wounded, perhaps even dead.

He broke the shotgun and stuffed two fresh shells into the breech as he ran toward the door. He slammed out into the hall and ran toward the door opening onto the outside stairway leading to the street.

176

With the shotgun at waist level, he plunged onto the landing. Most of the gang was hidden behind the corner of the bank building, but two were visible. Dan didn't even hesitate long enough to see who they were. He fired, one barrel at each, in rapid succession.

Smoke billowed out in front of him, almost obscuring the two and their horses. The roar of the double report was ringing in Dan's ears as he took the steps two at a time.

He broke the gun going down, and at the foot of the stairs, paused long enough to punch in two fresh shells. He whirled around the foot of the stairs . . .

Sarah was there. Her shotgun was broken open and she apparently couldn't get the spent shells to eject. Dan yelled, 'Forget it! Run for the alley! Quick!'

She glanced up, her face white with shock, her eyes filled with fear. There was a bloody stain on her upper sleeve. She dropped the gun and whirled. She tripped on her skirt and fell headlong.

Dan yelled, 'Get up! Move!' He whirled from her and faced back toward the street, gun ready in his hands.

The two horsemen at whom he had fired from the top of the stairs were down. Their horses had disappeared. One of the men was writhing in the street but the other was raising his revolver, taking aim . . .

Dan fired instantly. From a distance of

twenty feet, the entire charge of buckshot took the man squarely in the chest.

Only then did Dan see who it was. It was Rufus Wilkes, his uncle, and he was dead before he hit the ground.

Dan was sick at his stomach. But from now on there was no turning back. Sarah was hurt. Defending her, he had been forced to kill Rufus Wilkes. He would now kill whoever else he must.

There was still one load in his gun. Glancing around, he saw that Sarah was up, running, holding her skirts so that they wouldn't trip her again.

He retreated toward the alley, not daring to turn his back on the street. He knew Delaney was dead. He had seen him die. He supposed Cooper and Winslow were also dead. And Smead? He didn't know.

One thing he did know. All effective resistance to the gang had ceased. From now on, the town, the bank, everything was theirs.

He reached the alley and plunged around the corner. Sarah stood there, dusty, bloody, trembling violently, and weeping hysterically. She was now unarmed, and if she stayed here she would probably be all right. He said, 'You stay here!'

She didn't answer him. He turned his back to her and peered around the corner into the vacant lot.

He felt his revolver snatched from its

178

holster. He whirled to grab her, but she was running down the alley toward Fourth Street, the revolver in her hand.

There was a kind of insanity in her now, he thought. She was hysterical and almost out of her mind with fear, but her determination was unwavering.

He plunged after her. She rounded the corner into Fourth Street and ran toward the front corner of the bank. Dan could see several horsemen in the intersection. One of them was Sam. He was roaring orders at his men.

There was no gunfire in the street. But there was Sam's roaring voice, there was the noise of the gang's plunging horses. There was the crackling of the distant flames and the clang of the fire engine bell.

Sarah ran straight toward Sam and Dan knew what she meant to do. She thought he couldn't kill Sam and she intended to do it herself. Fifteen feet away from Sam Youngerman she stopped, and raised the gun with both hands, sighting it.

Sam's face turned toward her. He was a big man, a giant of a man. He looked like a child's conception of God sitting there on his big black horse. But suddenly Dan saw something in Sam's eyes he had never seen there before. It was something he had never expected to see in his oldest brother's eyes.

It was fear, the fear of dying, that same terror Dan had seen during the war in the eyes

179

of lesser men. And then Sam did something Dan had never thought could be possible. He raised his gun and pointed it at Sarah.

Dan's whole life had been spent in awe of Sam. Yet here he was, willing to kill the woman he professed to love to save himself.

Sarah was directly in Dan's line of fire. There was an icy ball in his chest. He leaped to one side raising the shotgun as he did. He raised it to eye level, knowing with cold horror that if he missed, Sarah would be dead before he could reload.

With Sam in his sights, he fired, and he saw the charge take his brother in the chest, driving even this giant of a man back like a great toppling pine.

Sam's enormous hands closed on the saddle horn and held him thus, upright in the saddle. But he was dead even as his horse galloped away wildly down the street.

Sarah stopped at the corner of the building. She turned her head and stared at Dan, wildness in her eyes. Dan stood exposed to the other members of the gang. In a moment they would riddle him just as they had riddled Delaney earlier.

But something unexpected was happening. Men poured into Main Street above the intersection. They were black with smoke and red faced from heat. Some of them carried axes and shovels, some carried guns. They had come from the east, where the fires raged now out of control.

They stopped in a ragged line that stretched from one side of the street to the other. They raised and sighted their guns, and the volley rolled out raggedly.

In front of the bank, the demoralized remnants of the gang stared with bewilderment. The first volley had largely gone wild. But the resistance offered by these angry men who had earlier abandoned their town to the outlaws had a greater effect on them than accurate bullets could have had. They glanced swiftly at each other and then, by common consent, whirled their horses and galloped away down the street.

Five lay dead, sprawled out in the dust. Farther down Main, Sam's body lay where he had finally toppled from his horse. Seven men, some of them wounded, galloped out of town.

The line of townsmen stared briefly at Dan and at the carnage in the street. Then they turned and hurried back toward where the fires burned.

Dan put his arms around Sarah, holding her trembling body close. They had lived here seven years, and all that time Sam had been an ever-present threat because they had known that he would come sometime.

Now the threat was gone—forever gone. Only this town remained, where they had spent the last seven years of their lives.

Dobeville was wounded now. Dobeville

181

needed help, and they were a part of Dobeville. Dan said, 'Come on,' and crossed the street, running, toward the place where he had last seen Sheriff Smead. Sarah ran after him, her dress still stained with blood, her face still stained with tears.

He glanced up and saw Cooper's frightened face peering down out of his window in the old Booth Hotel. Winslow grinned shakily at him from the other one. Across the street, Smead came limping out of the passageway, his face white and twisted with pain from a bloody wound in his leg.

Dan hurried toward him, to help him, feeling strong and sure of himself for the first time in a long, long while. This was their home and now would always be.

We hope you have enjoyed this Large Print book. Other Chivers Press or G.K. Hall & Co. Large Print books are available at your library or directly from the publishers.

For more information about current and forthcoming titles, please call or write, without obligation, to:

Chivers Press Limited
Windsor Bridge Road
Bath BA2 3AX
England
Tel. (01225) 335336

OR

G.K. Hall & Co.
P.O. Box 159
Thorndike, Maine 04986
USA
Tel. (800) 223-2336

All our Large Print titles are designed for easy reading, and all our books are made to last.